"Hard Rock Mountain"

M/M Straight to Gay First Time Romance

Jerry Cole

Disclaimer

Edition v1.00 (2016.08.10)
http://www.jerrycoleauthor.com

Chapter One

The cold, clear light of autumn shone through the mosaic of leaves like stained glass, lighting up shards of red and gold that trembled in the chilly breeze. Aspen trees, stark white and black-scarred, shook their scarlet leaves like ecstatic hands at the piercingly blue sky as though in praise of the foggy mountain peaks in the distance. In their shade, the grass was still vibrant emerald and starry with scatterings of hardy white wild flowers which the frost had yet to kill, growing right up to the rocky shore of the Gunnison River. Sunlight glittered and danced on the water's rushing surface, flashing on the bellies of leaping fish and the wings of birds darting to catch them. It was an awe-inspiring sight. Or it would have been, had Daniel been seeing it from almost any other situation but in watery glimpses while gasping for air as the furious current swept him violently downstream.

Freezing water flooded his lungs and tumbled him over and over until he couldn't tell up from down. The graveled bank scraped his skin as the rapids pitched him back and forth between rocks like the hands of a cruel and aggressive giant. He clawed frantically for any purchase, any respite or chance of rescue. For a moment, his fingers hooked in the shirt of another man, tossed on the waves with him. For just a second, their heads cleared the water and Daniel stared into deep blue eyes, huge with fear.

Then the current snatched them away from each other again. Daniel's head collided with rock and darkness consumed him.

Chapter Two

A month before, Daniel sat at his desk and wondered if he was happy with his life. He absolutely despised his work and loathed his empty, too small apartment. He hated being twenty-five and alone, looking into his future and seeing precisely nothing that excited him. Hate required a level of intensity Daniel just couldn't muster. Especially not right now when someone had dropped an entire quarter's worth of paperwork on his desk at the last minute again. Right now, at one in the morning after scrambling all day to wrench this company's finances into some semblance of recognizable order, he barely had the energy for breathing.

The office at night was an eerie, liminal space, rendered strange by its removal from the context of the work day. The only light came from Daniel's lamp and the wide windows that filled the south wall, providing a beautiful view of downtown which glittered like scattered jewels in the night. The office, dark and still, seemed like another planet compared to that shimmering nightscape. Empty desks and abandoned paperwork recalled something apocalyptic. A roach skittered from the shadows across the gray office carpeting, summoned by the promise of snacks forgotten in desk drawers. One of Daniel's coworkers had left their monitor on, and a twisting rainbow vector danced across his screensaver like a plastic bag caught in the last breeze through a forgotten civilization. Daniel watched it, and thought that he wasn't unhappy, just apathetic. Not content, just tolerating his situation for now.

Daniel was a master of tolerating things. For example, his boss. He laid his head on the cheap press board desk and the high lacquer cover reflected the light of the lamp and his own bored, chestnut colored eyes. He stared, dead-eyed, at the glossy brochure sitting near his cold coffee. It was full of colorful high resolution photos of gleaming trout and scenic mountain vistas. His boss had handed the little pamphlets out to everyone earlier, at the same time he announced the trip they were going to be taking to its advertised destination.

"Not just a company retreat, but the adventure of a lifetime!" the man had declared, scattering the brochures like confetti, "Hiking! Rafting! Team building exercises! This is just what we all need!"

Mr. Donahue was an...unusual man. Young to be in charge of such a large firm, but then his appointment had been blatant nepotism. His family had founded this company and helmed it for generations. Daniel could only assume that previous members of the Donahue clan had been a little more grounded. Their Mr. Donahue was more inclined to racking up huge expenses taking company cars out for extravagant dinners with clients and then vanishing to Tahiti for months at a time while everyone else scrambled to clean up his mess. To be honest, the office operated much better with him gone and not running around the building interrupting things with his 'innovative' new ideas for 'synergy' and 'drilling down to create high level scalable content with optimum bandwidth.' Daniel sometimes suspected Donahue just googled lists of those buzzwords.

6

He reached, hand limp with exhausted ennui, across the desk to drag the brochure closer, opening it up again. He'd glanced through the photos already, just long enough to be certain this trip was going to be offensively expensive and way more than the company could afford. Especially with the state their finances were in. He glanced at the stack of financial documents on his desk again and shuddered.

"I really think you should hire a proper CPA for this," he'd told Mr. Donahue earlier that day, "I'm not a certified accountant and I can't make heads or tails of this."

"You worry too much, Carter!" Donahue was a thin, dark haired man with a fashionable beard and a penchant for garish suits. Today's model was dark violet pinstripe. He had his feet, swaddled in Italian leather, propped up on his desk while an attractive secretary bent to light his cigarette. "Just sign off on it and send it down to records. They'll sort it out. That's what Johnson used to do."

Johnson had retired last year and Daniel had taken his spot, something he was now regretting. Johnson had been Donahue's go-to man and now he seemed to have decided because Daniel was in Johnson's desk, he would be performing all the same functions.

"Then records must have a much better grasp of tax law than me," Daniel complained, "Because this doesn't make any sense. There's money going everywhere, hundreds of unlabeled expenditures, paper trails that double back on themselves or just vanish...This looks like monkeys threw it together, Mr.

Donahue. If the company gets audited, you can't expect this to fly."

Donahue sighed dramatically and dropped his feet back to the floor, shooing away the secretary and putting out his cigarette. He grabbed one of the glossy brochures and shoved it at Daniel instead.

"Listen Carter. Daniel. Can I call you Daniel? You need a vacation. How long have you been working here? I don't think I've ever seen you take a day off! You're going to kill yourself, and stressing out about meaningless paperwork you were just supposed to stamp and mail out is not going to help you. What you need my friend, is white water rafting in the Colorado Rockies."

Daniel resisted the urge to roll his eyes, not taking the brochure. "Sir, with all due respect," he said, "I think I'll pass. I've got too much to do. And nature and I have never really gotten along."

"Daniel, I insist!" Donahue stood, shoving the brochure into Daniel's hands, "I need you at your best! And having a nervous breakdown over receipts is not your best! I expect you to go on this trip, have an amazing time, and come back refreshed and better than ever!"

"Mr. Donahue, really—"

"I said I insist Carter," Donahue repeated, leaning close enough that Daniel could smell his overpowering cologne. He spoke in a rapid fire monotone, "Seriously. You've racked up so many vacation days that it's starting to look bad. HR is getting on my case about it. If you don't take a week off, I will fire you. Is that clear?"

Daniel nodded rapidly and backed up, clutching the brochure.

"Good man," Donahue clapped Daniel on the shoulder cheerfully and returned to his desk, "Can't wait to see you there!"

Daniel, looking down now at the photographs of meadows erupting with vibrant wildflowers and beautiful rushing mountain streams so clear you could see the fish darting, flashing their rainbow scales, resigned himself to a week of misery. He'd never liked camping.

He packed up his things and made his way down the dark office hallway mostly blind, glad there was emergency lighting in the stairwells. He'd only ever been camping with his family, and his thoughts wandered back to those trips as he hurried down the stairs, trying to ignore the uneasy itch between his shoulder blades that the creepy stairwell and creepier parking garage gave him. His family had a talent for making what would be, for any other family, wonderful occasions for making happy memories, into Sisyphean trials worthy of the pits of Tartarus. Holidays, vacations, birthdays—there was nothing his family wouldn't or couldn't ruin. Sometimes it felt like they actively went out of their way to make things as awful as possible. Screaming at each other the entire time, refusing to plan so everything was rushed and half assed, complaining and dragging out old drama just to start fights... He felt exhausted just thinking about it. Or maybe he was just exhausted. Maybe camping as an adult would be different, but somehow he didn't think a bunch of coworkers he barely knew were going to be much better than his family.

He drove home, surrounded by the neon flicker of the city at night and glad he'd invested in the car. It was a pain having it in the city, but with as often as he stayed late at work and missed the last train, it was worth it. He climbed the stairs to his apartment alone and in silence, fumbled with the door keys, and watched the door swing open on his dark home. As he flipped on the lights, flickering fluorescents illuminating the bare little living/dining/kitchen area, he thought it was amazing how empty such a small place could feel. Everything was tidy. The furniture modern and soulless Ikea pieces that he'd bought more on price than because he actually liked them. It looked more like a sad budget showroom than a place anyone lived.

Maybe he should get a pet, Daniel thought, loosening his tie and hanging up his keys, bag, and coat on the hook by the door that was there for that purpose. He ran a hand through his black hair, mussed by the long work day from its neat, precise style, and noted that he needed to get a haircut soon. He wondered what kind of pet would he get, as he left the living area behind to enter the small bedroom where his bed invited him under its soft dove gray comforter. Dogs and cats were too noisy and messy. Same problem with birds. Fish maybe? Those always seemed more like decorations than pets. Possibly some kind of small rodent, fastidious and quiet, like a rabbit or a rat. But those needed a lot of socialization and he wasn't home that often. He could get a reptile, but he didn't want to be one of those guys living alone with a snake, and he didn't think he could handle feeding it anything alive...

He shed his clothes and folded them before he put them in the laundry basket, to keep them from getting wrinkled. He watched himself with impassive eyes as he brushed his teeth, thinking that he needed to work out more. He didn't look bad. He ate well, cooking on the weekends and bringing packed leftovers to work, and he swam at the community center a few times a week. But his body had always been inclined to be long and slender without much definition. Frustrating. He spat out his tooth paste and combed his hair. He'd never liked mirrors. They made him uneasy. When he was a kid, he'd had this fear that his reflection was alive and learning his expressions, and once it had learned them all, it would kill him and take his place. He always tried to keep a flat expression when he was in front of one, even today. Just out of habit. No one could have those kinds of childish fears at his age. He left the bathroom light on when he finished, its pale glow illuminating his dark bedroom.

He carefully removed the decorative pillows that had come with his comforter and sheet set and folded down the blankets before climbing in. It made it easier to make his bed in the morning. Having everything neat and organized and planned made life much easier. No less lonely though. He set his alarm and looked at the empty pillow next to his own. He didn't need a pet. But the other option was out of the question. He'd just have to get used to being alone.

Chapter Three

The next morning Daniel woke up on time, showered, dressed, ate his breakfast from the labeled Tupperware in the fridge, stuck a second labeled Tupperware into his bag for lunch, and left for work. It wasn't that he didn't want a relationship. He had tried before, many times. He wasn't bad looking and women liked that he had his life together. But it never worked out. He was too distant, they said, emotionally and physically. Never wanted to talk about himself. Always seemed disinterested in the bedroom. He might, more than one of them had suggested, be gay. That was ridiculous of course. Daniel would know if he was gay. Surely he would have noticed it by now. He wasn't into musicals or bodybuilding or anything else that his admittedly limited, mostly TV sitcom-based, knowledge told him gay people were in to. He was just a normal guy who prioritized his work over his social life like hundreds of other guys. He should try to at least make some friends, he thought. Maybe then he wouldn't want a relationship so badly.

The month leading up to the trip passed far too quickly for Daniel's liking as he endeavored to find any possible way to avoid going. He talked to HR, and it turned out Donahue hadn't been lying about him accumulating too many vacation days. They all insisted he take some time off rather than supplying any other option for how to get rid of them. He nosed around the office for some big, hard deadline project he could get involved in that would give him a reason to stay. But everyone on this floor was going on the trip as well and planning around it, and by the time Daniel got to asking people on other floors, rumors of his HR problem and the forced vacation had got around and they all adamantly refused him.

At this rate, he thought as he stood in line at the sporting goods store buying camping and hiking supplies, he was going to have to fake illness. He prepared for the trip anyway, of course. Daniel wouldn't risk going into it without everything he needed. He'd had that experience too many times. So he had researched, with exacting precision, everything he'd need considering the season and the climate in the Rockies and assembled a neat and affordable list, and then spent a frustrating night trying to figure out where to put all that junk away in his storage-challenged apartment. He'd donate it, once he got out of going on this trip, he told himself. Homeless people would love his unused, four-man tent and insulated sleeping bag.

The day of the trip approached like an execution date, grim and inevitable, it's slow progress towards him a source of increasing anxiety as he planned what he would bring and got his work taken care of and cleared away so that he wouldn't fall behind. He was still scrambling for a way out, wishing he still had any contact with his family so that he might claim an emergency on their behalf. Half wishing he could just get hit by a car on the way into work. Not fatally, just a little. A little car accident. Just enough to not have to go on this awful trip with his awful boss who wouldn't stop talking about it like it was the damn second coming, certain to heal all wounds and solve all problems.

The day before the trip, Daniel finally resigned himself to lying as a last resort. He hated it. Lying was abominable behavior. And even beyond the moral ramifications, he was no good at it. He'd never got a handle on how it worked. Still, he had to try. He called in to work from his apartment and claimed he was horribly ill—the flu or something—and that he was sorry but the doctor said he'd still be contagious for the next week so he couldn't possibly go on the trip and could they please convey his sincere apologies to Mr. Donahue? They'd bought it. They had no reason not to. He'd never taken a day off before, so it wasn't like they could suspect him of anything.

Afraid to leave his apartment and risk being caught in his lie, he parked himself on the couch with reruns of a cooking show and his laptop to finish up some work he could do from home. At least this day wouldn't be a total waste, even though his skin itched at the thought of the work he'd be unable to do while he was stuck here. Better a day than a week in the woods with Donahue. This might satisfy HR as well. It was a good plan.

The hours ticked by, the gentle murmur of the chef on TV failing to fill the emptiness of the apartment. This was why he never took days off. He hated being here by himself in the quiet. He'd rather be doing almost anything else. Anything except camping with Mr. Donahue. He turned the cooking show up louder and tried to focus on the spreadsheet in front of him. This would be over soon enough.

And then there came a knock on his door. A pit opened in the bottom of Daniel's stomach. He never got visitors. At best, it would be a salesman or religious proselytizer (he had never had any patience for religion), and at worst...

"Open up, Mr. Carter!" shouted an all too familiar voice, "It's the TLC train rolling into your station."

The pit in his stomach grew bigger. Daniel scrambled to pull the blanket over the back of his couch around his shoulders and affect the unhealthiest looking posture he could, shuffling over to the door. He'd barely turned the handle before Donahue and three secretaries (Two for form and one for function. The functional one's name was Susan and she had the patience of a saint and eyes like razor blades.) burst into his apartment with the kind of exuberance that implied confetti and music. Susan was carrying a crock pot which she took to his kitchen without another word while Donahue grabbed Daniel by the shoulders.

"There you are, the poor sickling!" Donahue laughed, pinching Daniel's cheek, "I heard you were ill! And knowing you, I knew it just had to be

15

something horrendous, so, being the excellent boss that I am, I decided to come and pay you a visit! Wasn't that nice of me! I even got Susan to make you chicken noodle soup!"

"It's minestrone," Susan corrected him, her voice as calm and unaffected as her suit was chic. "I don't do meat."

The other two secretaries were opening his blinds and windows to let in the sunlight. Daniel, stunned by the sudden rush of activity, could only stare for a moment.

"You really shouldn't have," he murmured, pulling himself together, "I'm contagious. I don't want to get you all sick as well—"

"Nonsense!" Donahue spun Daniel around and frog marched him back to the couch while Susan fixed a bowl of the soup. "We're going to have you back on your feet and glowing with health in time for the camping trip tomorrow, or my name isn't Edmond Ignatius Donahue! Now eat your soup."

True to his word, Donahue spent the entire day practically glued to Daniel's side, commenting every few minutes on how much healthier Daniel looked already.

"A medical marvel!" he declared around nine when he and the secretaries finally gathered themselves to leave. "You look as good as new,

Carter. I'll see you bright and early tomorrow for the trip!"

"Of course, Mr. Donahue," Daniel agreed, too exhausted to fight, just waiting to close the door behind them so he could have some peace.

As Daniel was closing it, Donahue caught the door and fixed a steely glare on his employee. "Do not be late, Carter," he said, his voice as flat and severe as the desert. "Do not."

Daniel swallowed a nervous lump in his throat, agreed, and closed the door. After all that, the silence of an empty apartment was almost preferable.

Chapter Four

He spent the evening in abject misery, packing up his camping supplies for the trip and resigning himself to the inevitable. In the morning, he considered just 'getting caught in traffic.' But somehow he was certain Donahue would hold the plane or worse, come and pick Daniel up himself. The man was a lunatic and for some reason he'd fixated on getting Daniel to go on this trip. HR couldn't be bothering him that much, could they?

So he woke bright and early, moved his things to the car, and drove to the airport where he was meeting the rest of his coworkers going on the trip. There were around ten of them, most of the people who worked in his office, minus a few who had successfully come up with excuses. Daniel knew only a few by name. Jacobs, who always refilled the coffee pot in the lounge. Lynda with a 'y', who wanted to go by her first name and had about thirty potted succulents on her desk. Fitz, who had issues with time management and panicked at deadlines. He had never been social at work and rarely bothered to learn anyone's name. Maybe that was something he should work on, he pondered, staring into his overpriced airport coffee and thinking about his empty apartment. Making a few friends would be better than being alone, and probably healthier than trying to pin all his needs on a romantic relationship that was bound to fail. He eyed Lynda over his coffee. She'd always seemed friendly. Maybe if he started a conversation...

He was still trying to work up the motivation to try when Donahue and the secretaries arrived. Susan carried the bags, balanced in her slim arms as though they weighed no more than feathers. Donahue, with no respect for the peace of an early morning airport, was as noisy and exuberant as ever, dressed like a lumberjack going on tropical vacation.

"Carter! You made it!" he cheered when he saw Daniel and hurried forward to pull him into a very unprofessional and unwanted hug. "I told you that you were over that little cold! You're going to have a great time buddy."

He clapped Daniel on the shoulder so hard that Daniel suspected bruises, then went on to greet the others. Shortly afterwards, the plane was boarding. Donahue and the secretaries were flying first class while the rest of the team was in coach. Daniel had expected no less. Daniel hoped in an idle, nervous way, that he might be seated beside one of the office mates whose name he knew, and might have a chance to try talking then. Unfortunately, the aisle seat next to him was occupied by someone not from the office at all. Daniel flew in silence, listening to Lynda and Jacobs a seat ahead of him exchanging gardening tips and talking about Jacobs's kids. He felt lonelier than ever.

It wasn't a long flight and there were no layovers. Daniel dozed or read and before he knew it they were leaving the airport for a hired bus. Daniel was one of the first out of the terminal, having packed and prepared well while Donahue was having a fight about his carry ons, so it surprised him to see someone already waiting when he got on. There was a man near the back of the small charter bus. He was sleeping, brown suede ranger hat tipped over his face, his arms up over his head and his feet on the seat in front of him. He was huge, Daniel noted, with tanned skin and brawny muscles. His eyes lingered on those arms, envy a brief green sprig in his heart, wishing he could look like that. The man dressed neatly but casually in a blue button up that strained over his impressive chest, and jeans over boots. Beneath the rolled up sleeves of his cotton shirt, Daniel could see the dark edges of a tattoo. It wasn't difficult to guess that this man didn't work in the office.

Daniel leaned back to check with the bus driver that this was the correct shuttle and the heavyset woman assured him it was and that, no, she didn't know who the guy was either. Daniel sat down to wait for the rest of the team and decided to put the stranger out of his mind for now. He yawned, groggy from his flight, and pulled out his book again.

He'd only been reading it a few minutes before a low voice spoke into his ear. "What're you reading?"

Warm breath against his ear and the brush of stubble against his cheek. Daniel nearly flew out of his seat in his haste to turn and see who was so close to him, staring in confusion when he saw the stranger in the seat behind him, leaning over the back, smiling with a kind of lazy amusement at Daniel's reaction. He had the kind of ruggedly handsome face women and Hollywood adored, though his nose, which bore the evidence of repeated breakings, was probably too crooked for a career in movies. His hair was blond, a golden contrast against his bronze skin. A pale white scar cut through one of his brows, curving up from his right eye, which was exactly the sharp, piercing blue of an autumn sky. Plus, with the hat, he had exactly the look of some kind of good for nothing cowboy. Daniel's heart raced, wondering how such a huge guy had got the drop on him. Slowly, he eased back into his seat and tried to settle his breathing.

"Just a novel," he answered, trying not to stammer. "Sci-fi thing."

"I like sci-fi things," the man replied with a lackadaisical air and a mild drawl. "What's it about?"

Daniel eyed the man, wondering what his motivation was.

"Pretty standard," he replied, "Humanity makes contact with aliens for the first time, but it's the first time meeting another intelligent race for the aliens as well, so there are lots of misunderstandings. The story follows a human diplomat trying to prevent interstellar war."

Daniel had expected the guy to lose interest fast, but instead he just grinned. "Sounds like a trip," he extended a hand for Daniel to shake. "Asher Price."

"Daniel Carter," Daniel replied with a confused frown, shaking the man's hand. "Are you here for Mr. Donahue's trip?"

"In fact I am, Daniel Carter," the man squeezed Daniel's hand before he let it go, and Daniel's heart jumped in a way he couldn't explain. "Will the boss man be here soon?"

"He had some trouble with his bags, I think," Daniel answered. "He'll be a little bit."

"That's fine," Asher shrugged, standing and moving around to Daniel's seat. "Mind if I wait here with you for him?"

Daniel moved over as Asher sat down, not waiting for an answer, close enough for Daniel to feel his body heat. He didn't have the courage to tell the man no, but he suddenly wished he did.

They sat in silence for only a moment before Asher broke it again.

"So what are the aliens like?" he asked.

Daniel looked at him, brow furrowed, for a moment, trying to gauge how serious he was being, then answered.

"Bugs. Bees, for the most part. Though the winged males are humanoid."

"Ah, so it's that kind of sci-fi book."

"What does that mean?" Daniel blushed, defensive. It was definitely that kind of book. He enjoyed them, as long as they had a good plot to back up the smut. Asher just laughed, seeming to enjoy Daniel's flustered expression. Other members of the office began filtering onto the bus and Asher was quiet again for a bit, watching for Donahue. Daniel tried to go on reading, but was having difficulty focusing with Asher so close.

"So does she forge a political marriage with one of the winged males to save both planets?" he asked after a bit.

"I haven't finished it yet, but probably not," Daniel replied, "I think she's just going to run off with the alien military commander. She doesn't seem to have much investment in Earth. That's why she went on the mission to meet the aliens in the first place."

"That's unusual," Asher's eyes were still on the window, waiting for Donahue to appear from the terminal doors. "Usually the people in those stories are all about getting home as fast as they can."

"Yeah, I guess that is pretty different."

"I can sympathize," Asher grinned, but there was something not entirely happy behind it. "I'd like to leave this place behind myself sometimes."

Before Daniel could respond, Donahue swanned through the terminal doors, complaining loudly and bitterly about how he'd been treated. Asher was on his feet at once, patting Daniel on the shoulder.

"Be right back," he said, and winked. "Hold my seat for me."

By now most everyone was already on the bus and settled down, or Daniel would have made an effort to get someone else in that seat immediately. Something about the stranger unsettled him, and his talkative streak was only part of it.

He watched through the window as Asher hurried up to Donahue, who stopped on the sidewalk to meet him, frowning with more seriousness than Daniel had ever seen on the boss's face. They talked for a few minutes before Donahue, expression sour, headed past the man towards the bus, and Asher followed. By the time he reached the bus doors, Donahue's charismatic grin was back in place.

"Alright! Is everybody on?" he asked, clapping his hands. Asher pushed past him to reclaim his seat next to Daniel, and Daniel made room for him, wishing he'd been brave enough to move to another seat.

24

"Settle in! It's about an hour and a half from here to Estes Park."

Daniel glanced at Asher and told himself he could definitely handle this for an hour and a half. It wouldn't be so bad. He just wouldn't talk. If there was anything he could do, it was not talk.

"Before we get going," Donahue continued, "I'd like to introduce you all to Mr. Price. He'll be our trail guide for the duration of our visit. He's a very experienced ranger so if you have any questions be sure to direct them to him."

He indicated Asher with an elaborate gesture, then sat down. Daniel eyed Asher, thinking that made more sense than any of the possibilities he'd been considering. Asher looked like the rough wilderness survival type.

"So, tell me more about the book," Asher said as the shuttle pulled away from the airport.

Daniel sighed and offered the book to the other man.

"Here, why don't you just read it yourself?" he suggested. "I brought another."

"Nah, no thanks," Asher waved it off, shaking his head. "I don't read."

Daniel wrinkled his nose in utter bafflement.

"Just tell me when you figure out if she's going to go back to Earth or not," Asher said, then leaned back, pulled his hat down over his face, and went to sleep, dozing off almost at once. Daniel was regretting this trip already.

Daniel read a little more before he too began to doze, his head against the window. He dreamed of reaching the campsite only to discover he was the only one who'd brought a tent and had to share it with everyone. Including the trail guide, who was cramming himself in as close to Daniel as possible, asking specific and probing questions about books Daniel hadn't read while all ten of his coworkers and Mr. Donahue piled into the tent on top of Daniel, slowly crushing him.

Chapter Five

As the bus jerked to a stop, Daniel woke and blinked back to awareness, realizing his left cheek was no longer pressed against cold glass, but rather his right was resting on warm skin. He frowned down at the muscular chest he was lying on, not yet conscious enough to figure out what was wrong with this picture.

"Comfy there, friend?"

Connecting two and two, Daniel jumped away so quickly he came close to head-butting Asher in the chin, embarrassment coursing through him like fire in his veins.

"Sorry," he gasped, unable to look at the other man as he all but flattened himself against the window. "I must have fallen over in my sleep. I'm so sorry."

Asher just chuckled.

"It's nothing to turn so red about. Happens all the time. Relax before you give yourself a heart attack."

"It won't happen again."

It was as much an apology as a promise to himself.

"Yeah, better save it for the trip back," Asher's smile wrinkled the corners of his blue eyes in a way that just made them more magnetic. "We're here."

Daniel turned quickly to look through the window behind him, and saw that they had pulled into a parking lot in the town of Estes Park, eastern gateway to the Rocky Mountain National Park. Donahue had paid the shuttle driver to bring them directly to the entrance where a hired park service truck was waiting to bring their gear to the campsite. Daniel hurried to get off the bus and away and from Asher, thinking about how much this had already cost the company. He wondered if Donahue was even keeping track. Somehow he doubted it. Donahue was too used to just throwing money at things and expecting there to always be more.

Daniel moved his things from the bus to the truck with his usual efficiency, and then waited for everyone else to catch up. The employees would be walking behind the truck while Donahue and his secretaries rode with the driver. Fortunately it wasn't a very long way, and Daniel had the foresight to dress for a walk in a collared shirt under a patterned wool cardigan. Light enough that the sun wouldn't bother him, but enough layers to keep out the cold. He thought he looked quite nice, though Donahue, dressed like a rock star on African safari, had scoffed at him.

They gathered behind the truck at the end of the road which rolled out ahead of them past a pair of gate houses and vanished into a sea of endless greenery. Daniel looked up into the early afternoon sunlight to catch a glimpse of the distant silhouette of mountains, hazy and impossible in the distance, just lilac shadows against the too bright sky. They were still close to the road and the noise of civilization, but that would vanish soon, swallowed up by the insular layers of pine and cottonwood, replaced by the twin rush of wind and water and ever-present bird song. Even now that airy music was beginning to make itself known. It could not overwhelm Donahue playing some too energetic pop song on his phone and laughing loudly, stirring up the other members of their little group who he decided were not excited enough.

"There's space in the back for you, Mr. Price!" Donahue called as he climbed into the truck, patting the luggage stuffed bed invitingly as he swung up into the cab. Daniel looked back to where Asher was ambling up to join him, expecting the trail guide to accept and climb on, but Asher shook his head.

"That's alright. I'll walk," he called back, putting an arm around Daniel's shoulders and catching him by surprise. "I've got a conversation I wanted to finish with Daniel here."

Donahue raised an eyebrow, looking at Daniel with a curious, calculating stare, but then he shrugged, pulling a secretary into his lap and signaling the driver. The truck headed into the forested entrance and the office workers jogged after them.

"You have something to say to me?" Daniel asked, frowning, as they started walking.

"Not really," Asher shrugged. "I just can't stand that guy. What an asshole."

Daniel laughed, half in surprise, finding himself in agreement with the trail guide for the first time.

"He's the worst," Daniel agreed.

"Oh yeah?" Asher asked. "Not a fun boss?"

"Not at all," Daniel huffed at the thought. "He has no idea how to run a business, so he just pushes the work off on to everyone else. He spends company money like it grows on trees and expects people to just sign off on his receipts anyway. He basically forced me to come on this trip—"

"Whoa there, cowboy," Asher laughed, patting Daniel on the shoulder. "I'm starting to sense maybe you don't like the guy very much."

"Sorry," Daniel cleared his throat, realizing he'd let himself get carried away. "I guess I'm a little bitter. I really didn't want to come today."

"Not a fan of camping?"

Daniel gave Asher a sidelong glance that clearly read 'look at me, do I look like I camp?' Asher smiled, shaking his head.

The trees, fir and pine with their dark bones and birch all stark whiteness, closed over the paved road into the park quickly as jaws, enclosing them in a green arboreal world. It was amazing how fast the sounds of the road were left behind. Even in this late season, the park was still full of life. Elk and fox and alpine birds, unbothered by the cold, made their subtle stirrings in the wood around them. Or at least Daniel imagined they did, until a moment later when he began to see tents and RVs—the roar of their generators obscene—and realized just how densely populated the shallows of this forest sea were. The campers here were like shoals of fish over the reef, only a degree removed from the civilization they were more comfortable with. Daniel hoped things would be quieter deeper in. A fat squirrel scurried across the road ahead of them, a fast food wrapper in its mouth.

"So why'd he force you to come?" Asher asked, making small talk as they passed through the camping area and moved on uphill further into the park.

"Who can tell what goes on in his head?" Daniel muttered, watching a gaggle of children chasing each other with water guns. "He claims it's because HR was getting on to him for my accumulated vacation days."

"Not the type to take time off?" Asher asked, catching Daniel's shoulder and pulling him out of the way of a stray blast of water. "Why's that?"

Daniel shrugged Asher's hand off and scowled at the children, a little embarrassed and unsure why he was confiding in this weird guy. Was he really that lonely that he'd open up to the first friendly person? His prickliness had usually chased people away by now. Daniel was inclined to give Asher more of a chance just for sticking around this long.

"I don't have the most active social life," Daniel answered, pausing halfway through the sentence as he considered the best way to word it without it sounding as pathetic as it felt. "Not a lot of friends."

"More of a family guy?" Asher wagered, raising his eyebrows. Ahead of them the old truck sputtered and roared as it made its way up a steep hill. The gaggle of office workers trudged up after it with similar noises.

"I don't talk to my family," Daniel said, tone clipped, making it clear that was not a subject he wanted to discuss. "I would just rather be at work, getting something done. Sitting at home by myself feels pointless."

"Makes sense," Asher nodded, and then looked at Daniel with a thoughtful frown. "Your family. Do you not talk because you're gay?"

Daniel stiffened, instantly defensive. A crow was startled off a nearby branch by their passage, mirroring Daniel's feelings with a loud, outraged caw.

"I'm *what*?" he repeated, hoping the color on his face could be explained by the brisk wind tugging at his hair. "I'm not gay!"

"What, you didn't know?" Asher asked, smiling conversationally as the breeze tossed his long golden hair around his face like something from a romance novel. "It's pretty obvious if you ask me."

"Based on what?" Daniel squeaked, almost more offended by how casual Asher seemed to consider this conversation than he was by the assumption. They'd fallen a little behind the rest of the group, still puffing their way up the steep hill.

"You're a well-dressed loner with better personal hygiene than most women I've met, and you were reading a romance novel on the way here," Asher replied, chuckling and shrugging like he was commenting on the weather and not such a deeply personal part of Daniel's life "You're either gay or a serial killer."

"I'm *not* gay!" Daniel repeated, adamant and bewildered by the turn this conversation had taken.

"Serial killer it is then."

"Fuck you!"

The condemnation burst out of Daniel like the cap exploding off a shaken bottle of soda. The froth of hurt and anger threatened to continue spilling out, but Daniel shoved it back down quickly and bottled it away. He hurried forward instead, humiliated, eager to put some distance between himself and the other man, who still seemed smugly amused by the whole situation. Daniel couldn't believe he'd been fooled into conversation with that ass for even a minute and regretted his own desperate unpleasantness for making him lonely enough to not have rejected that guy at the start. Somehow he wasn't surprised at all that the one person his social awkwardness didn't drive away would be someone even worse than him. Declaring him gay just because he dressed nice—who did that? He'd just have to spend the rest of the trip avoiding the trail guide as much as possible.

They soon arrived at the campsite, and Daniel began setting up his tent at once. Mr. Donahue was organizing the building of an absurdly large fire pit, already pontificating loudly on everything he wanted to do this week, most of which ranged from ill-advised to unquestionably illegal. Daniel made certain to set himself up a good distance from the others. The site where they were camping, Aspenglen, was nicely off the road and fairly open, but there was enough tree cover that Daniel found a sheltered spot near the back without much difficulty. His tent was easy to set up and, after reading the instructions, Daniel was finished quickly, arranging his belongings neatly inside just to eat up a little more time before he would have to go out and socialize. He sat inside his tent, dawdling to avoid having to go out there. At least the campsite was nice. When he closed his eyes, beyond the laughing noises of his coworkers, he could hear the rush of the mountain wind through the trees, the caw of a crow, and the distant eerie bugle of an elk somewhere higher up the mountain. And the rustle of nylon much too close. He frowned, opening his eyes, and peered out of his tent curiously.

Asher was directly across from him under the same tree, setting up his own tent.

"Is that you, Freddie Mercury?" Asher asked with a teasing grin as he staked down his tarp, "What a coincidence. I guess we're neighbors."

Daniel pressed his lips together into a thin line and counted to ten until he could control his breathing again. Deciding it was better to say nothing, he zipped his tent closed again and hid until he heard Asher finish setting up and head over to the fire. He had known this trip was going to be a disaster.

After a little while, he worked up the willpower to leave the tent, ambling out towards the fire reluctantly. The sun wasn't even down yet, but the fire was already huge, the campers clearly just having a good time burning things. They were going to end up in trouble with the park ranger, Daniel thought. Maybe he'd get lucky and they'd get kicked out, and this awful trip would be canceled early

He put in an appearance near the fire long enough to earn himself a couple of hot dogs, then retreated to the edge of the festivities were he felt more comfortable. There was a log seat which looked out on the astounding view their camp site had afforded them. The mountains seemed to go on forever, blurring into the foggy distance. It was almost unsettling to think about how old they were. They'd been here long before his oldest ancestor was born. They would be here long after he was gone. It was a humbling thought, those lonely gray stones in the distance, standing silent sentinel over the earth forever, long after everything living today had turned to dust.

"Should have guessed you'd go for the sausage."

Asher, the glow of the fire on his bronze skin making him look even more impossibly attractive than earlier, plopped down on the log next to Daniel. Daniel felt his jaw clench in immediate outrage.

"Is there a reason you're harassing me?" Daniel asked, words clipped and frigid. "Or do you just derive enjoyment from acting like a school yard bully?"

"Maybe I just felt bad for you, seeing you sitting over here by yourself?" Asher suggested with a shrug, taking a bite of his burger.

"So you decided to cure my loneliness with homophobia," Daniel's lip curled and he looked away, agitation palpable. "Good idea."

"I find you interesting," Asher confessed with a shrug. "That's all. Not my fault you're easy to tease."

"It's not teasing," Daniel snapped, standing up. "And I don't appreciate it. Go bother someone else."

Daniel threw away his half-eaten hot dog and went to bed early, tossing and turning in his sleeping bag for hours before he dozed off, and not just because Donahue turned the bonfire into a drinking party as soon as the sun was down and kept the noisy celebration going long into the night. He couldn't stop thinking about the trail guide and his obnoxious insistence that Daniel was gay. He wasn't! There was simply no way. He would know by now. He'd been with women, after all. Even enjoyed it sometimes. So sex had never been as amazing as everyone seemed to think it was, and the thought of being with a woman like that had never really grabbed him the way it had other guys. That didn't mean he was gay. He just had a low sex drive. He was just a normal guy. He told himself this as many times as he needed to in order to relax and fall asleep. It took a while.

Chapter Six

Asher did not take the hint. The next day, they hiked up Deer Mountain and Asher stayed near Daniel the entire time, making 'teasing' comments between pointing out birds and local features to the rest of the group.

"If you look on that branch there you'll see a blue tit. Guess you wouldn't be interested in that, eh Carter?"

"The elk pass through here in the summer. When the males are in rut, they'll travel miles and climb mountains to find a partner. I'm sure you know what that feels like, Carter."

And so on, the entire several mile hike. By the end, Daniel wanted to tear his hair out or cry or maybe just punch Asher right in his smug face.

He restrained himself with great effort, doing his best to remember that this was only going to be for a few days. Once this trip was over, he'd never have to look at that obnoxiously roguish grin ever again.

The second day out, they headed to one of the many lakes to swim and picnic. Donahue had some sort of temper tantrum about wanting to go rock climbing, but Susan managed to talk him into giving them all a rest day in between the long hike yesterday and the next activity. Daniel couldn't fathom how she managed to control him.

Daniel brought a book and sat on the rocks with his feet in the water to read, enjoying the cool day and the beautiful view. The water was clear and shining in the distant white early autumn sun, the rocky shore warmed by its light. The mountains painted everything with a majestic backdrop, curving up around them like they were sheltered in the hands of a huge, stony giant. It felt strangely safe. The yellow leaves of birch trees drifted on the wind and the smell of snow from the mountain tops was fresh on the air.

"So, did she go back to Earth?"

Daniel groaned, hiding his face with his book, as Asher swam up to the rock Daniel was on.

"Don't be like that," Asher laughed, "I'm going to control myself today, I promise. Seriously, I'm interested."

"She didn't," Daniel answered tersely, pulling his legs up in the not entirely irrational fear that Asher would drag him into the water. "I'm not to the end yet, but she's told the alien commander she wants to stay with him."

"Ah, man I'm glad," Asher pulled himself up onto the stone with almost no effort, the powerful muscles of his arms flexing. "I was worried she'd have some kind of reversal and decide Earth was her true home after all."

Daniel stared as Asher climbed up beside him, watching the water run down his chest like something out of one of those risqué cologne commercials. A layer of glistening water highlighted every ridge and hollow of the man's incredibly well built body. He had far more tattoos than Daniel had expected from what he'd seen peeking out from under his shirt. He seemed to favor geometric black work, his chest below his collar and his arms halfway down his biceps covered in an interlocking pattern of hexagons and crisp dark lines with areas of complete black. It was beautiful in a very stark, modern way, totally at odds with the down-to-earth, nature-loving attitude Daniel had seen from him so far. At least until he looked closer and realized there were animals woven into the sharp designs. Ravens and deer picked out in dot work, hidden among a forest of abstract shapes.

"Enjoying yourself?"

Daniel realized he was staring and quickly averted his eyes. Asher laughed.

"It's fine," he said. "The tattoos, right? I wouldn't have put so much work into them if I didn't want people to stare. Don't worry about it."

Daniel allowed himself to look back, trying to ignore how small the swimming trunks Asher was wearing looked. Daniel hadn't bothered to put on a swimsuit at all, relaxing in a t-shirt and shorts. Given tacit permission, Daniel went back to staring at the tattoos.

"They're amazing, actually," he said, only a little grudgingly, part of him not wanting to give Asher the satisfaction. "I've never seen anything like it."

"Been working on them since I was eighteen," Asher admitted. "Worked hard to afford 'em. They have a lot of meaning to me. You have any?"

Daniel shook his head.

"I considered it when I was younger," Daniel admitted. "But I couldn't think of anything I cared about enough to wear it the rest of my life. Plus, time and money..."

He shrugged, not bothered by missing out on it. He was still mostly ambivalent to the idea, even if seeing Asher's tattoos made him wonder what it might be like. Asher let the subject trail off. Daniel finished staring and went back to his book.

"Not swimming, I take it?" Asher asked.

"Too cold," Daniel replied. "I don't feel like getting sick on the second day of a week-long trip."

"You're missing out." Asher pointed to where his coworkers were clearly having a great time, their shouts and laughter carrying over the water as they drifted on floats and splashed water at each other. Lynda and Jacobs were dunking each other, clearly hitting it off. They'd probably be sharing a tent before the end of the trip. That could end awkwardly.

"If I'm missing out, so are you," Daniel reminded the trail guide, who just smiled and stretched out on the rock, letting his skin dry in the sunlight.

"Nah, I'm having a great time," he said, smiling and closing his eyes.

Daniel shook his head. What an endlessly confusing person. He went back to reading and shared a peaceful hour or more in near silence, trading only a comment or two when Daniel got up to fetch them sodas. If he could be like this all the time, Daniel thought, Asher wouldn't be half bad.

The next day, they prepared for a second hike, a longer one, up Lawn Lake trail. Donahue had decided they would not only hike up there today, but then raft back down Roaring River. Daniel was not positive that was safe or allowed, but Donahue had never really cared about either of those things. There was a river and he wanted to raft it.

The walk was pleasant and the hike was not a difficult one. The land scaled fairly evenly up towards the Mummy Range. Lawn Lake was nestled right between Mummy Mountain and Fairchild Peak. Daniel couldn't help wondering who named these places. The first part of the hike was through forest, and Daniel enjoyed that the most. The path hugged close to the side of the Roaring River, clear water rolling noisily past them over mossy stone. Birch and cottonwood leaves in shades of scarlet and gold were carried on the river's current, executing complicated dances as they circled each other, swirling towards oblivion. The air was sweet and full of the scent of cold water and growing things. Elk were calling somewhere not far away, and small, wary life shuffled in the leaves just out of sight.

Daniel thought he would have enjoyed this hike and this whole park a lot more if he hadn't been there with so many other people. He just wanted to relish the peace and quiet of the gorgeous place. But his coworkers could never seem to stop talking. It was always something. Would it really be better to be alone though, he wondered? Neither option appealed. The most attractive concept was still just to go home.

Soon enough, Asher was dropping into step beside Daniel. Daniel eyed him warily, wondering if it would be the genial Asher of yesterday or the teasing bully of the day before.

"You're looking good today, Elton John," Asher said immediately, answering Daniel's question. "Are those new boots?"

"They are," Daniel replied with an irritated sigh. "I bought them for the trip."

"You're going to regret that." Asher looked off towards the path ahead, smiling at the sight of a bird darting across. "If you don't have blisters already from the Deer Mountain hike, you will by the end of this one. New boots have to be broken in before you wear them on a hike like this."

"I can handle a few blisters," Daniel walked faster, trying to put a little distance between them, but Asher just lengthened his strides to keep up. "After all, I can tolerate you."

Asher snorted, shaking his head. "Hey, you're no prize yourself," Asher pointed out. "You could be a little friendlier."

Daniel rolled his eyes. "You declared me gay five minutes after meeting me and have been using it as an excuse to throw homophobic insults at me ever since. Forgive me if I don't exactly respond to that kind of treatment with warmth and acceptance."

Asher had the gall to look offended, recoiling with a frown that became anger a second later.

"Hey, I was trying to be nice to you—"

"Well, you failed. You might want to re-examine what exactly you think constitutes nice behavior."

"I guess you'd rather just spend this entire trip by yourself?"

"Yes, actually, I would," Daniel bared his teeth at Asher in a vicious smile. "Being alone for the rest of the week would be infinitely preferable to another minute with you."

Asher looked taken aback, but he dropped it, turning and stomping away while muttering curses under his breath. Daniel breathed a sigh of relief. Maybe he had finally got the man off of his back.

The trail continued up into the forested foothills of the mountains. The Roaring River gushed and babbled beside them, full and noisy. Beautiful, but looking entirely unfriendly to raft. Daniel swallowed, thinking about trying to ride down that thing. Donahue was going to get them all killed.

The sun rose towards the middle of the sky as they climbed higher and, when he didn't think about Asher or the trip back down, Daniel began to genuinely enjoy himself. The trees and plant life were beautiful, the day was cool and pleasant, and the view was spectacular. He ran his hands over the pale white trunks of birch trees and watched the vibrant leaves spiral down ahead of them like something out of a fairy tale. A tunnel of autumn arches sheltered them, instants of bright blue sky blossoming between brown branches whenever the wind stirred.

Daniel paused as they reached a high point in the trail to look away, catching a glimpse of an elk through the trees, carefully picking its way through the underbrush. He watched in silence, appreciating the quiet moment as the rest of the group pulled ahead, leaving him behind.

"Oh, how pretty."

Daniel looked up in surprise when he heard someone speak, realizing Lynda had stopped to watch as well. She kept her voice soft so as not to startle the animal, and they watched together as it nosed through the leaves and pine needles.

"This has been so great," she said with a happy sigh. "I really needed this. It's been so long since I got to be out in nature."

Daniel felt suddenly in over his head. She was trying to be friendly and start conversation, and all at once it was like he'd never talked to another human being before. He scrambled for a topic.

"It seems like you and Jacobs are getting along," he said, then immediately regretted it, afraid he'd overstepped polite boundaries.

"Yeah," she sighed wistfully. "It's not going to work though. He's still in love with his ex-wife."

"I'm sorry to hear that," Daniel said, and meant it. Doomed relationships weren't great conversation starters.

"How are things with you and that trail guide?" Lynda asked suddenly, giving him a saucy, sidelong glance. "I noticed he's been following you around since we got here."

Daniel grimaced. "It's not like that," he said. "*I'm* not like that. I don't think he is either. He's just an asshole who's decided it's entertaining to harass me."

"Really?" Lynda seemed surprised. "Do you think there are people who would spend that much time just on bothering someone?"

"Absolutely."

Lynda shrugged, looking back towards the elk.

"Maybe he's one of those immature guys," she said. "The kind who never figured out yanking on a girl's pigtails isn't the best way to get her attention."

"If he could get to be our age," Daniel replied, tone dry as the Sahara, "and still not have figured that out, then he's definitely not someone I'd want to be dating. Even if I was into guys. Which I'm not."

"You know you don't have to be so closeted," Lynda patted him on the shoulder consolingly. "It's 2016. I'm pretty sure the office would accept you."

"Uhg," Daniel huffed, clapping a hand to his face. "I'm not closeted! I'm not gay! I wish people would stop assuming things. Especially when I tell them flat out it isn't true."

Lynda took a step back, surprised by his vehemence. The elk, startled by Daniel's voice, darted away deeper into the woods.

"Sorry," Lynda sounded like she meant it, brows furrowed in concern, but then she pressed her lips together and glanced after the group. "We had better catch up. They're getting pretty far ahead..."

She hurried away, leaving Daniel to stew in his regret. So much for this trip being his chance to make friends. He didn't want to be so prickly and unpleasant all the time. So why did it always seem to happen anyway?

He caught up with the group, but stayed near the back, not yet ready to try socializing again just yet. Maybe there was some book or manual out there everyone else had read on how to successfully have relationships, and he had just missed it somehow. He couldn't think of any other reason he'd be so inept at this.

Chapter Seven

Gradually, the deciduous trees thinned out, replaced by evergreens as they got higher. In places the trail was entirely obscured by a bed of pine needles, thick and fragrant and soft underfoot. Eventually, the pine began to thin as well, and the path wound through a cleared, rocky valley beside a deep, glittering lake. Daniel breathed deeply, the air cold and clearer than he'd ever tasted in the city. What a beautiful place.

When he looked around, he saw the group spreading blankets near the lake shore. "Are we stopping for lunch?" he asked someone.

"I guess so," she answered. "At least until Mr. Donahue gets back."

"Mr. Donahue?" Daniel frowned. "Where did he go?"

"He and the secretaries got tired of walking," Daniel's coworker replied with a shrug. "They decided to stop and wait for the truck Donahue hired to bring the rafts up here."

"Of course he did." Daniel sighed, rubbed his eyes tiredly, then went to find a place to sit and eat where he could look at the water and not think about his annoying, incomprehensible boss.

He considered, for a moment, asking Lynda if he might sit near her to eat. But remembering the look on her face when he'd snapped at her earlier, he decided not to bother. Instead he sat apart from the others, eating an unsatisfying sandwich alone. At least the view was beautiful, he reminded himself. And he'd only have to put up with this for a few more days. Who was he kidding? He'd have to put up with the loneliness the rest of his life probably. He stuffed more peanut butter and jelly in his mouth and tried to ignore his feelings.

He glanced at the others again and noticed Asher wasn't with them. He must have decided to take the truck with Donahue after Daniel scared him off. Was he really just trying to be friendly and being horribly bad at it? Daniel supposed it would be hypocritical to judge Asher if that were the case, considering his own difficulties with socializing. No, he thought a moment later. No way! There was no way a man that handsome and charismatic could possibly be that bad at socializing that he would think insults were an acceptable form of conversation. The man was just a garden variety asshole. That was all.

Daniel had just finished his sandwich when he heard an engine and looked up to see a suped-up four wheeler hauling a trailer full of rafts clattering up the trail. Asher was driving, Donahue behind him, while the secretaries clung to the bouncing, rattling trailer, looking decidedly unhappy about their situation.

"There you all are!" Donahue called, waving to the group, "I hope you're ready for some intense white water rafting! This is going to be fantastic."

Daniel wasn't paying much attention to Donahue's cheerleading. His attention was preoccupied by Asher, who looked more upset than Daniel had ever seen him. The man's face was set like granite in a fearsome scowl, his jaw clenched, and his eyes hard. He was glaring daggers into the back of Donahue's head as Donahue organized the unloading of the rafts. He looked like an entirely different person without the lazy, teasing grin Daniel had grown used to.

There were three rafts, each one big enough for five people. Donahue and his secretaries quickly claimed one and the rest of Daniel's office mates split between the other two. Daniel dawdled, unsure which one to try claiming a seat in. Should he try to sit with Lynda, who he'd offended earlier today? Or was it better to sit with people he'd never spoken to before at all? Unable to decide, he realized too late that both boats were full and he was standing next to Asher, contemplating the long hike back down.

"Looks like you two will just have to take the spare!" Donahue laughed, pulling a last, much smaller and more worn looking orange rubber raft off the truck. It was just big enough for two. Daniel looked at Asher, preemptive misery already building like storm clouds on the horizon. Asher was still just glaring murderously at Donahue. What had the other man done to spoil Asher's mood so drastically?

"That's fine," Daniel said, taking the orange raft and beginning to drag it towards the mouth of the river where it left Lawn Lake. "Let's just get this over with."

When they got back to camp, he was giving up. He would just sleep in his tent the rest of the trip and wait for this to end. Asher said nothing, only stormed after him in tense silence.

"You first, you first!" Donahue pushed Daniel and Asher towards the water ahead of everyone else. "You're the guide, after all!"

Daniel eyed the water. It was running fast even here, and on the way up, he'd seen how shallow and furious it swept over the stones. He looked at Asher, hoping the other man would put stop to this madness. Instead he just tossed his bag into the raft and started wading out with it, grunting at Daniel to get in. Daniel, swallowing his nerves, obeyed, throwing in his bag as well and scrambling in after it. He looked back anxiously, and suddenly realized there weren't even any signs posted. If this was the Roaring River, shouldn't it have a plaque or an info board, like every other rock and tree of any significance in this park?

Asher climbed in as soon as Daniel was settled, Daniel holding onto the stony shore to keep them in place as he did so. He could feel the current tugging hard at the boat, eager to pull them away. When Asher was seated, Daniel let go and the raft shot off at once, the rest of the group dwindling quickly in the distance. Daniel looked back and watched them recede, suddenly worried.

"Focus, Daniel," Asher snapped at him, steering them around a rock with his oar. "I'm going to need your help with this."

"Right. Sorry," Daniel grabbed his own oar to assist in steering them down the rapid current. "This will slow down eventually, right?"

"I sure hope so," Asher muttered as they both paddled frantically to avoid an overhanging branch.

"What do you mean you hope so?" Daniel asked, the other man's flippancy bothering him. "Haven't you done this before?"

"Hell no," Asher confessed. "I just went along with your crazy boss."

They crashed over a small fall, water rushing over them and temporarily making speech impossible.

"You're the trail guide!" Daniel shrieked when he could speak again. "It's your job to tell him when things are too dangerous!"

"What gave you the idea I could tell that asshat anything?"

"No one can tell him anything, but you could have at least not gotten right into the water like it was fine!"

They slammed into a rock, and Daniel fell against Asher's broad back, nearly dropping his oar. The raft scraped over it and kept going, the current too fast for them to slow down from one collision. Daniel looked back but couldn't see anything through the spray. Was it just him or was the raft deflating?

"Are the others behind us?" he asked. "Should we try to slow down?"

"We can't!" Asher said loudly as Daniel straightened up and struggled again to paddle in time with him. "If we try to go against this current we'll just end up spinning."

"Really?"

"Probably!"

"Have you ever been rafting in your life?"

"No, actually! Shut up!"

"Shut up?! I'm going down rapids with a trail guide who's never rafted before!"

"Yeah! So you should probably let me focus!"

Daniel laughed bitterly, mocking himself and his own luck as much as he was mocking Asher.

"I should have known," he laughed, voice cracking "I should have figured it would end up this way. I knew this trip would be a disaster from the beginning."

"If you could *not* do your whole pretentious pessimism thing right now," Asher grated out as they scraped over more rocks, catching actual air for a moment before hitting the water again with a teeth-rattling slam, "that would be great!"

"It's your fault it's been so awful!" Daniel snapped. "You can at least do me the favor of letting me complain about it!"

"Why should I?" Asher snarled back, narrowly shoving them away from another rock. "You made it clear as crystal my opinion doesn't mean a damn thing to you when all I ever did was try to make conversation with you. I guess there's a reason you're always alone—no one can fucking stand you!"

"Yeah well I never asked you to take pity on me, did I?" Daniel threw his oar down into the boat, too angry to focus on their situation. "I never asked for shit except to be left alone! And what the hell is your problem with gay people anyway?"

"What makes you think I have a problem with gay people?" Asher turned to stare at Daniel in utter, furious bafflement. "I AM-"

"ROCKS!" Daniel shouted, uselessly, a second before their raft collided with the jagged stones and

55

flipped over, sending Daniel, Asher, and their bags flying into the rushing water.

Chapter Eight

Water.

Filling his lungs and his eyes and his ears. The roaring of the river and of his pulse when he slipped below. Snatches of sky. Brief desperate gasps for air quickly choked as the water pulled him in again. The bruising pain of rocks slamming into him over and over. A pair of deep blue eyes reflecting his own fear back at him.

A moment of peace, liquid suspended, infinite black above him and shimmering blue below, like drifting in the upper atmosphere. In the dark, the currents pulled him in a strange waltz around Asher, both of them reaching for each other through the void. They spun around one another like the leaves that drifted on the surface, weirdly serene. Their fingers brushed and then were wrenched apart. Peace vanished as Daniel sunk.

Then darkness, and a vast nothingness which Daniel expected never to end. This was how he was going to die. Fighting with a homophobic trail guide on an ill-advised camping trip he had done his damndest to avoid. What would his parents think when they heard the news? He imagined they'd be sad. He wasn't close with them, but they were still his parents after all. But maybe after a little while they'd be relieved not to have to think about him anymore. He'd always felt like they only put up with him out of obligation. Just staving off their own guilt...

There was warm pressure on his lips and a lump in his throat that rose and spilled out of him in a great, hacking cough. Someone was gripping his shoulder, turning him onto his side as he vomited river water in wracking gouts that left him shaking and dizzy. His entire body ached like he'd been beaten with a sack full of rocks. Which, Daniel realized as he remembered the river and acknowledged that he was still alive, was basically what had happened. How wasn't he dead? He struggled to focus his vision and saw the blue eyes that had haunted his trip down river staring at him in concern.

"There you are! Stay with me. You can't pass out again, alright? You have to stay awake."

There was an arm around him, cold as his own skin, dragging him up to his feet. He tried to put his weight on his right ankle and felt it buckle. He didn't recognize his own voice when he cried out in pain.

"I know, I know," said a voice in his ear, drowning out someone babbling about how much it hurt, which he belatedly realized was him. "Just lean on me. Just a little further. You can do it, buddy. Keep your eyes open. Just focus on me. I'm right here..."

The world faded out again for bit, then someone was shaking him by the shoulders, forcing him back into wakefulness.

"What did I tell you about passing out? You have to stay awake!"

"I'm trying," Daniel mumbled, his vision swimming. "I'm sorry. I'm trying."

"It's alright. Just keep talking to me. Tell me what you can remember."

"Rafting. Rocks. Hit my head."

"Further back than that. What's your name? Where did you grow up?"

Daniel shook his head and then regretted it at the flare of pain that brought. He still couldn't seem to focus properly. There was someone in front of him, looking at his hurt ankle. Those blue eyes were staring right through him.

"Daniel," he answered, and was surprised when he had some difficulty dredging the information up. "Carter. I grew up in...Central Florida. My parents... Dad was a contractor. Mom had...a lot of jobs."

His head started to bob again and then someone was shaking his shoulders again, making him open his eyes.

"Come on, keep talking! Memories, Daniel. Uhh...family Christmas! Go!"

"Grandparents' house, till they died. Could smell candied nuts a mile away. Family screaming at each other over every stupid thing. Always hated loud noises. Hiding in the yard till I got frostbite, wishing it was over..."

"Count backwards from ten for me Daniel."

"10, 9, 8, 7- AH!"

There was a sudden sharp pain in his arm. The world snapped into relief. He swore, vehemently and blasphemously, kicking at the rocky ground under him as fiery pain lanced through his shoulder and down his arm, burning as it went. Asher was in front of him, still holding Daniel's wrist and shoulder, his expression fraught with worry.

"What the hell was that?" Daniel asked, hunching over as he became aware of pains all over his body. He'd never felt this bad in his life. There wasn't an inch of him that didn't hurt.

"Your shoulder was dislocated," Asher explained, letting go of Daniel with a sigh that spoke of both relief and exhaustion. "I got it back in."

"Shit," Daniel whined, holding his screaming arm. "That was the one part of me that didn't hurt."

"Yeah, you're welcome." Asher grumbled, and then made a wheezy, fluttery pain sound that was so unlike him Daniel was temporarily distracted from his own distress.

"I'm afraid I'm gonna need you to return the favor now," Asher said, moving his jacket aside. Daniel felt nausea boil in his gut as he saw a rough black pine branch embedded in Asher's side. Asher looked pale.

"It's not deep. But I can't..." he paused to breathe, clearly struggling, "I can't get it out myself. And if I pass out without bandaging it, I'll bleed to death. I need your help."

"Are you crazy?" Daniel shook his head. "We have to get you to a hospital! We can't take care of something like that out here!"

Asher took another series of strained breaths. "Look around."

Daniel obeyed. They were in a clumsily constructed lean-to, just loose pine fans leaning against the side of a large rock, rapidly thrown together a few feet from the river. Outside, the sun was setting scarlet and turning the rushing water red. The silhouette of mountains beyond the river was not the same as what Daniel remembered seeing from Lawn Lake or from where the Roaring River ended at Horseshoe Park. But that didn't make sense.

"I don't know where we are," Asher gasped. "But it's getting dark. It's going to be awhile before anyone finds us. And I don't want to wait around and see if this punctures something important the minute I move wrong. Okay?"

Daniel took a deep breath, forcing his nerves to steady.

"Okay," he said, though he could hear his pulse pounding in his ears. "Okay. We can do this. What do I need to do?"

"There's a first aid kit in my bag there," Asher tipped his head to indicate the battered, waterlogged packs that must have washed up with them, "Get the gauze, bandages, and disinfectant ready."

"You don't think a puncture like that is going to need stitches?" Daniel asked, eyeing the branch uneasily. It was thicker than his thumb.

"You know how to suture a wound?" Asher asked, blinking as his vision unfocused. Daniel could tell he wasn't going to stay conscious much longer. "Yeah, it needs stitches. But I'm really hoping we'll make it back to a hospital before it becomes critical. For now, gauze and bandages."

Daniel nodded and began digging through Asher's soaked bag, surprised to find the man hadn't waterproofed things better considering they were going rafting. Daniel had secured everything he brought with him in a double layer of plastic bags, predicting a dunk in the river as inevitable. He'd been more right than he could have ever anticipated.

Fortunately, the case the first aid kit was in was watertight and he opened it to find the bandages still clean and dry. He brought the kit over to Asher, stomach churning as he looked at that wound again.

"This is going to suck," he said, and Asher snorted.

"You're telling me."

Daniel took a deep breath, already resigned to this and past the point of being afraid of it. This had to happen and he was the only one who could do it. Daniel wrapped his hands around the end of the branch and looked at Asher for confirmation that he was doing the right thing. Asher, white as a sheet, licked his lips, braced himself against the rock, and nodded. Daniel pulled.

The branch slid free with a distressingly wet sound and a howl of pain from Asher. Daniel cast it away, not wanting to look at how much of the length was covered in Asher's blood. The trail guide swooned, groaning, and slumped towards the ground.

"Hey, hey!" Daniel caught the larger man, lowering him down more easily. "Don't pass out! Stay with me!"

But Asher was already gone, overwhelmed by the pain. Daniel cursed, his attention pulled back to the now open, gushing wound. He didn't have time to wait on Asher to regain consciousness. He'd just have to do what seemed right. He poured disinfectant over the injury, hoping there weren't any splinters still embedded in there, and then packed the hole with gauze, shuddering as it soaked through almost at once. He secured the packed gauze with bandages, wrapping them tightly and hoping the pressure would help keep Asher from bleeding out too fast. When he was done, he sat back, covered in the trail guide's blood, and wondered what he was supposed to do next.

He looked down at himself, taking a mental inventory. His left ankle was swollen and throbbing. Sprained at least, if not fractured. He had a feeling he had more than one fracture to worry about. His entire body felt bruised. Worst of all were the ankle, his shoulder, and his head where he'd hit it on the rock. There was blood crusted in his hair there, which made him shudder in disgust. He contemplated going to try and wash, but he didn't want to leave Asher alone for even a minute right now. Instead he wiped the other man's blood off his hands onto his shirt the best he could and dug into his pack for something to eat.

He watched Asher anxiously as he chewed on a granola bar, hoping the trail guide woke soon. He'd never thought he could be so desperate for the company of such an irritating person, but the concept of being alone out here was terrifying. He'd take Asher's grating presence a million times over being stranded here by himself. He'd probably be dead if the trail guide hadn't hauled him out of the river, and that was something he didn't really want to think about. If he'd hit that rock just a little harder they would both be dead.

Daniel shivered and looked out through the limited shelter of the pine branches. They must still be fairly high up, he thought, because the forest outside was all evergreen from what he could see. The firs trembled in the chill evening wind, shaking fragrant needles at the bruise colored sky. An owl was calling in the distance, the sound soft and velvet. Daniel cocked his head to hear it better, wondering where it was, and what other animals might be in the area.

The sun was sinking lower all the time, casting bars of gold through the black pine branches and illuminating the deep carpet of red needles, and the temperature was dropping with it. He was no wilderness expert, but he was smart enough to know that being in these soaking wet clothes at night out here was a death sentence. He finished his granola bar quickly and then dug through both packs. He found a rechargeable emergency lamp and set it up against the rock, illuminating their miserable little lean-to against the coming night. He had brought a change of clothes, safely bagged and dry, and he found one of those emergency foil blankets in Asher's bag. Asher had also brought a sleeping bag, rolled up at the top of his pack and thankfully still sealed in its watertight packaging from the store. He also found fire starting equipment, which was soaked, and which Daniel didn't begin to know how to use. He left it aside to dry out and started pulling off his wet clothing instead. As he awkwardly attempted to get his shirt off without further agitating his incredibly painful shoulder, he heard Asher shift behind him.

"If you're trying to cheer me up with a strip tease, kid," Asher joked, his voice weak with pain and

65

exhaustion, "I appreciate the gesture, but I'm not really in the mood."

Daniel didn't dignify that with an answer, just continued struggling with his damp shirt.

"Thanks for not letting me bleed out," Asher continued, and he sounded sincerer than Daniel would have expected from him.

"Can you move enough to get your own clothes off?" Daniel asked through chattering teeth as he cast his shirt aside. "We need to get dry or we're going to freeze."

"Please tell me you're going to warm me with your naked body. That's hilarious."

"Freeze then!" Daniel snapped in irritation, struggling with his belt while he shivered. "Don't you think this situation is awful enough without your bullshit on top of it?"

"Relax," Asher sighed, and Daniel heard his voice waver with his own shudders of burgeoning hypothermia. "Just trying to lighten the mood."

"You could try helping instead," Daniel grumbled. "You're supposed to be the expert. I don't even know how to start a fire."

"You're doing fine," Asher sounded surprisingly reassuring, despite the pause to shiver in his words. "You're right about the clothes. But moving isn't really something I can do right now..."

He trailed off as Daniel, victorious over his stubborn belt, began removing his pants, his back to Asher as he slid them carefully over his injured ankle, hissing at the pain. All that was left was his underwear, as soaked to his skin as everything else. He turned to glare over his shoulder at Asher.

"Don't look." he said pointedly and the trail guide, still lying on his back against the rock, held up his hands in innocence and turned his face away. Daniel peeled off the wet underwear and cast them aside with his other wet things. He'd had a small microfiber towel with his clothes, not much bigger than a washcloth, but he dried off with it as best he could, then pulled on the dry underwear from his spare clothes. He wondered if he shouldn't put on the entire outfit, but he didn't want to get them damp from what he couldn't dry off, and Asher had a point about person-to-person warming. Wasn't skin to skin supposed to be the best way to warm up? Did that still work when both people were wet and cold?

Putting off deciding, he turned, mostly naked, back to Asher, who was watching him with a smile on his face.

"I told you not to look," Daniel hissed, but Asher just shrugged. "Whatever. We need to get the wet clothes off of you."

"Be my guest," Asher offered, shivering even as he gestured down at himself like he was welcoming Daniel to an all you can eat buffet. Daniel rolled his eyes in irritation and, moving carefully as much due to his own injuries as to Asher's, he began removing the trail guide's clothing, trying not to focus on the other man's eyes watching him while he peeled away the damp flannel of his shirt. Daniel hesitated as he reached Asher's pants.

"Don't get shy now," Asher teased. But Daniel could see how hard the other man was shaking in spite of his playful grin. The blood loss must be making his temperature drop even faster than Daniel's. They needed to move quicker. If Daniel could yank a branch out of this man's side, he could take off his pants. He fumbled with Asher's belt for a moment, then began tugging his jeans down, doing his best not to jostle the other man. Still, he heard the hisses of pain Asher struggled to hide, raising his forearm to his mouth and biting down to muffle the noise.

Eventually, he succeeded in getting the wet pants removed, guilt eating at him from the pale, strained look on Asher's face. All that was left was his underwear, unfortunately tight clinging white boxer-briefs, which Daniel decided not to remove, as he had nothing to replace them with. He patted Asher down with the towel as much as he could, then dragged the foil thermal blanket and the unzipped sleeping bag over the other man. He even threw the sweater from his dry clothes on top just for every extra degree of heat he could get. Asher was staring into space, close to passing out again. Daniel, with only a moment's trepidation, started to lie down next to him.

"Wait."

Daniel jumped as he felt a cold hand on the small of his back.

"There's no point if we're lying on the ground," Asher mumbled, his words a bit slurred from cold and exhaustion. "It'll leach all the heat."

Daniel hummed anxiously, but it made sense. He considered his options for a moment before taking the sleeping bag and spreading it on the ground.

"Do you think you can move enough to lay over here?" Daniel asked, though Asher's eyes were closed, his shivering weaker now.

Accepting that the other man was helpless, Daniel shifted closer to put his arms around Asher, swallowing hard with nerves as he wrapped himself around Asher's muscular, tattooed chest. As carefully as he could, he shifted the trail guide over, off of the ground and onto the warm fleece lining of the sleeping bag. Asher didn't respond except to groan in pain at the movement. Daniel propped the other man up on his side where his injury would hopefully be in the least danger of being rolled on in the night. Finally, Daniel lay down, his back to Asher's chest, and pulled the foil thermal blanket over them.

Asher's skin was cold against Daniel's, clammy with lingering moisture. He could feel the other man shivering and knew he was as well. Daniel hoped he was doing this right. It could kill them both if he wasn't.

"Asher?" he whispered as the night sounds outside their inefficient little shelter echoed around them. "Please don't die."

Asher didn't answer. Daniel, feeling small and afraid, huddled against the other man and tried to sleep.

Chapter Nine

Exhaustion and injury were powerful combatants against the fear and anxiety that tried to keep Daniel awake. Soon he was sleeping hard, dreaming of being back in that river, sinking into fathomless cold depths alone. He reached for the surface, but it was always beyond him, and he couldn't swim fast enough to reach it. Sometimes he would get close enough to the shimmering silver underside to see people above the water, moving somewhere beyond him. He tried to call out to them, but water flooded his lungs. Someone was staring down at him, but they wouldn't reach out. He strained for the surface desperately, the shifting shattered silver mirror reflected light just beyond his fingers, and found it solid as glass. He was under ice and there was no way out. Slowly, realizing the truth, he stopped moving. He sank slowly into the darkness, unresisting. The figure on the other side of the glass watched him, silent and unmoving.

He woke early, the light of morning still gray, the sun not fully risen from behind the horizon. He felt cold and stiff and his injuries ached, but he was alive and warm.

He realized with abrupt embarrassment that he could feel every inch of Asher's body pressed against him. The larger man was all but molded to Daniel's back, an arm around Daniel's waist. Daniel could feel Asher's breath against his scalp, the trail guide's face buried in his hair. They were as close as lovers, though no lover Daniel had ever had. As he stirred, trying to figure out how he could get out of this embrace before Asher woke up, he felt the other man's arm tighten around his waist, squeezing him closer. Asher sighed, breath warm against the back of Daniel's neck.

"Would you look at that?" Asher yawned, holding Daniel no less tightly. "We're still alive."

"We're probably not in danger of freezing anymore," Daniel replied, hunching his shoulders. "So if you could let go of me..."

"I don't know. This is kinda comfy."

Daniel struggled, squirming, until Asher released him, laughing. Daniel sat up, injuries complaining loudly, and regretted it as soon as the blanket slid off of him, shivering hard in the early morning chill. There was frost on the pine needles of their lean-to, and Daniel's breath fogged before him as he scrambled for his dry clothes, pulling them on as quickly as he could. He'd laid out their wet things the night before, but when he touched them he found them still damp, unsurprisingly.

"Here." Daniel threw his sweater at Asher, figuring he could get by better on the shirt and undershirt he'd packed than Asher could get by naked. Asher, still lying down, probably trying not to disturb his injury, caught it and gave Daniel a grateful nod.

Daniel watched the other man struggle to put it on as he gathered up the wet things.

"Stay there and rest," Daniel said. "I'm going to hang these clothes up somewhere the sun will reach them and see if I can't figure out where we are."

"Take your time," Asher's voice was strained as he finished putting on the sweater and lay back down again. "I'm not going anywhere."

Outside, a chill autumn morning was spreading slowly over the mountains. Silver mist made a slow, stately procession through the pines, just black cutout silhouettes in early morning obfuscation. The dawn lights gilded the eastern faces of the distant peaks in gold and dripped down into the valleys, running in the flashing currents of the river. Birdsong and the scent of sap and wet stone rode the breeze to Daniel's ears and nose, but there was no trace of any man made thing. No shout of voices or roar of car engines. No sign that there was any other human being on the planet but Daniel and the injured trail guide behind him. Daniel frowned at the splendor of nature, worry turning his stomach. He hung the clothes over a low branch where they could dry, hoping it wouldn't take long.

"See anything?" Asher asked as Daniel returned. Daniel, shaking his head, dug a granola bar and a water bottle out of the bags instead, handing them to Asher before taking the last granola bar for himself.

"That definitely isn't the Roaring River, though," Daniel said, sitting down. "That would have dumped us right in the middle of the camping area. Even if we were only part of the way down it, we should be able to see Lawn Lake trail. So we must be somewhere else. Does Roaring River have any tributaries we could have been washed down?"

"I don't think so," Asher squinted, trying to remember. "I mean, I think there's a river near Lawn Lake that cuts through Black Canyon, but if we'd gone through Black Canyon I'm pretty sure we'd be dead. The river through Black Canyon drops 35 feet per mile. It's one of the steepest drops in America."

Daniel frowned, remembering the brochures he'd read to prepare for the trip. "Wait," he said, "Isn't that Black Canyon in Gunnison National Park? I thought the Black Canyon here was a different Black Canyon?"

Asher looked bewildered. "Aren't they the same thing?"

"How should I know? You're the trail guide!"

"Well why the hell would there be two Black Canyons in Colorado? That's intentionally confusing people!"

"Don't yell at me, I didn't name them!"

"Whatever!" Asher threw his hands up, struggling to sit up so he could eat their paltry breakfast. "I'm eighty percent sure we didn't go through a canyon."

"Then where did we go?" Daniel asked, rubbing his suddenly tired eyes. "If we were in the Roaring River, we can't have just magically teleported into a different one."

"Well then, the most obvious answer must be that we're still on the Roaring River," Asher suggested. "And we're just in some weird little obscure bend. If we follow it a mile in either direction we'll probably find the trail."

"I don't think we can walk a mile right now," Daniel observed, thinking of his own twisted ankle, not to mention the hole in Asher's side.

"No, and we're not going to," Asher shook his head, leaning against the rock as he opened his water bottle. "It just means it shouldn't take the search party long to find us. So we're going to stay put and wait."

Daniel nodded, agreeing that seemed like the best course of action. Even if they'd somehow ended up in the Fall River or anything else, if they were by a major body of water like this, they'd be easier to find.

Asher continued to rest lying down, and Daniel took it easy near him, not wanting to strain his sprained ankle more. But he felt too restless to hold still for long. Soon the sun was up properly, melting the frost and turning the day more pleasantly cool.

Daniel felt grimy, the blood crusted in his hair making his skin crawl every time he felt it. Eventually, with a huff of irritation, he gave in to his need to get up and do something, taking the empty water bottles and limping out of their little shelter to check on the clothes.

The river was calmer here than it had been up at Lawn Lake. Which is why they'd washed up instead of being swept further on, Daniel assumed. It ran cheerfully down over the stones, heading deeper into a valley between the distant peaks, swallowed by forest. Daniel refilled the water bottles first, then ran his hands over the clothes, smiling when he saw they were mostly dry now, wool smelling of sunlight and pine.

He should collect them and bring them back to the lean-to, but his eyes were drawn to the river instead. He was wary of getting back in, afraid of the cold, of getting swept away. But the current seemed gentle here and he was dying to feel clean. He debated with himself for a few minutes before giving in. He took off his clean clothes and set them aside, not wanting them to get wet. After a moment of hesitation, he even removed his underwear. Asher was incapacitated and there didn't seem to be anyone else around to see him, so he might as well have dry underwear when he was done.

He stepped into the cold water and shuddered, rethinking his plan at once. But he was already naked and in the river now—there was no point in going back. He began splashing water onto his skin, washing off the blood and dirt. He bent to wash the blood out of his hair, cursing as the cold water hit his scalp. At least it seemed to be a warm day. He wouldn't freeze while waiting to dry off. He sighed with relief when he could run his hands through his hair without hitting any clumps, though now he could feel the outline of the split in his head where he'd hit the rock. It curved up the right side of his scalp like a false part, and continued past his hairline, ending just above his eyebrow. He'd probably end up with a scar there, knowing his luck. One more thing to keep people away.

"Looking good there, Carter!"

Daniel turned abruptly as he heard Asher's voice, seeing the other man leaning against a tree and watching him openly, still wrapped in the sleeping bag. Daniel scowled through his blush.

"What are you doing up?" he asked, harsh with annoyance as he hurried to get out and fetch his clothing. "You're not supposed to be moving. If that wound starts bleeding again—"

"I'm fine," Asher seemed equal parts exasperated and pleased by Daniel's concern. "Couldn't just lie there all day. Thought I would come and get dressed. Plus, you've been gone for a bit. I got worried."

Daniel, grabbing his clothes and moving behind a waist high rock for a little privacy, noticed Asher had collected his own clothes from the branch and removed Daniel's sweater.

"You might as well clean off first," Daniel said, indicating the water. "No sense getting all that grime on your dry clothes."

"Good point," Asher nodded. "But let's be honest. You're just trying to get me naked again, aren't you?"

"Whatever satisfies your grossly overinflated ego," Daniel rolled his eyes in disgust. So they were back to these jokes again. He made a point of not looking as Asher set the sleeping bag aside and crouched in the shallows to splash water on himself, trying to avoid getting his bandages wet.

Daniel lingered behind the rock, letting the sun dry him a bit more before he put on his clothes, feeling much more refreshed now that he was clean. While Asher finished washing and dressed, Daniel rolled up the sleeping bag and returned it to its waterproof canvas, tucking the foil space blanket in with it. He was just tightening the straps on it when he heard a twig snap. He looked up, expecting to see Asher, and instead saw a huge, shaggy face.

The bear stared back at Daniel placidly, blinking its huge brown eyes, motives inscrutable. It was so much bigger than Daniel had ever imagined bears to be, or maybe it just felt that way because he was standing in front of it. The sunlight shone on its glossy fur, and it looked fat and healthy, ready for the coming cold season. Daniel backed away slowly, not taking his eyes off the animal. He was sure it didn't consider him food. As long as he wasn't a threat, he would be fine. These were justifications he would mostly make later. In truth, his mind was blank, reciting a litany of swear words as he moved on instinct. He heard the bray of a cub a second before it ambled past its mother towards the water's edge. Daniel could feel his heart in his throat. His mouth was dry as cotton. Just keep backing away, he thought. Don't give it any reason to consider you a threat. Everything is fine.

"HOLY SHIT," Asher shouted behind him. Daniel's heart stopped cold as he glanced back at the other man, standing by the river bank behind him, pale with fear as he saw the bear. Daniel's attention was quickly drawn back to the animal as he heard it give a low warning bellow, rising up on its hind legs threateningly, six feet tall and looking down at Daniel with an animal's cool, unreadable gaze as it decided whether it was going to kill him or not.

"Shit, run!" Asher shouted, and Daniel didn't need any further encouragement. He turned and bolted, loping awkwardly on his injured ankle. Asher waited to catch him and the two men supported each other as they fled, looking back at the bear as it ambled after them with a furious bellow.

Daniel clung to Asher like a life line, terror coursing like ice water in his veins and his ankle screaming. He didn't dare stop or even look back at this point though, too afraid a moment's hesitation would mean an angry mother bear shredding him into a series of terrified ribbons. Asher seemed equally scared witless, half holding Daniel up, half using him as a crutch, neither of them in good running condition. Regardless, they kept running blind, sprinting into the forest while the bear's bellows echoed behind them. The sleeping bag, slung over Daniel's shoulder, bounced against his back like a warning.

And then, so suddenly Daniel had no time to do anything but gasp, the earth vanished beneath their feet and they were sliding down, tumbling, rolling head over heels through scrub and rocky scree, sliding down the mountainside. Every impact jarred Daniel all the way through to his bones, making every injury he already had even worse. Daniel waited for the crash, the coming dark, but the slide just seemed to go on forever, and then just as suddenly, it slowed. Daniel rolled to a gradual, conscious stop, and wished he had passed out. He had never hurt so much in his life. His hand was still clutching Asher's shirt. He hadn't let go of the other man even as they'd fallen. Daniel looked up at the sky through the gap in the trees that swayed above them, and regretted everything.

"Is the bear still coming?" Asher asked, weak and muffled by gravel. He was face down, but clearly in too much pain to move. Daniel struggled to move enough to look up at the sloping ravine they'd just rolled down. He saw no sign of the bear.

"I don't think so," he said, letting his head drop back onto the ground.

"Good," Asher said through his mouthful of rocks. "In that case, I'm just gonna lay here and bleed for a little bit."

"Good plan." Daniel agreed.

They laid there, catching their breath and feeling their new injuries for a while. Daniel was covered in new cuts and bruises. He didn't think there was an inch of un-lacerated skin on his body. *Honestly, fuck nature*, he thought.

"Your side," he turned his head towards Asher, ignoring the stringent complaints of his neck. "Is it bleeding again?"

"Probably," Asher shrugged, then groaned in regret.

"We should change the bandages," Daniel sighed. "I can't let you survive all of this just to bleed out."

"The first aid kit is in the bag," Asher replied. "Back up the cliff. With the bear."

Daniel swore, long and colorful, hissed vehemently into a tussock of scratchy mountain grass near his face. By the end of his tirade, Asher was wheezing with pained laughter.

Slowly, leaning on each other heavily, the two men recovered enough to stand and stumble towards the cover of the trees, squinting at the wilderness around them in bewilderment. Daniel kept a careful grip on the sleeping bag, the only gear they had anymore, glad he'd had the presence of mind to hold on to it, and that he'd packed the foil blanket into it earlier. The canvas had been torn by rocks on the way down the mountain, but the bag seemed mostly intact. A few rips were better than no protection from the cold at all.

Asher had saved one of the water bottles, and they passed it back and forth as they walked, somewhat aimlessly, trying to find a way back up the cliff towards the river. Neither of them wanted to discuss what they would do if they somehow managed to find the camp again and the bear was still there. Eventually, as the sun got higher in the sky, they had to accept that following the cliff was not leading them back to the river, only further up the mountain.

"If we keep going, we're bound to hit a trail eventually," Asher, looking pale and uncomfortable, tried to reassure Daniel. "There isn't an inch of this place that hasn't been landscaped for the tourists."

"What about those big swathes on the map just marked 'wilderness?'"

Asher pressed his lips together and breathed out heavily through his nose.

"We'll be fine," Asher said through gritted teeth. "We'll find a trail and we'll be fine."

"Right." Daniel agreed and didn't say anything else for a while as they continued their stumbling progress into the forest, making their way up the hill.

"We'll get to a high point," Asher suggested after a time, still looking for a plan to deal with this. "From above the tree line, we'll be able to see the landmarks and figure out where we are."

Daniel didn't have a better plan, so he went along with it, until he realized blood had soaked through Asher's bandages and was beginning to stain through his clothing.

"Okay, time for a break," Daniel said, leaving no room for argument as he let go of Asher and sat down. Asher tried to protest, but it was obvious he could barely stand without Daniel's help right now. He sank down at the base of a tree, closing his eyes. Daniel took a moment to stretch out his sprained ankle, glad to have his weight off of it. The walking had become almost unbearable. When the flaring pain had settled to a dull throb again, he shifted closer to Asher, lifting up the other man's shirt to check on his bandages.

"You really don't get tired of seeing me shirtless, do you?" Asher joked. Daniel ignored it, scowling.

"This is bad," he muttered. "We really need to get you proper medical treatment."

"I'll make it till we get rescued," Asher said, looking pale and tired. "We just have to get back to the river. It looks worse than it is, I promise. I can walk, right?"

"You probably shouldn't be walking, though," Daniel frowned, concerned. "When we find the river again, or any big body of water, we're stopping and you're not moving again until we get help."

"Okay, Mom," Asher teased, chuckling. "Whatever you say."

"How about you stop making dumb jokes and focus on figuring out where we are?" Daniel shifted away from Asher again, leaning against his own tree to rest. "You must have some idea. There's only so many places the river could have dumped us."

"Yeah, you're right," Asher took a deep breath, closing his eyes again as, Daniel assumed, he tried to remember all the rivers in the park. "But there really aren't any branches off the Roaring River. And we can't have been swept down to Fall River, or we'd have drifted right through one of the main camping areas. So the only thing I can think is... Maybe we weren't on the Roaring River to begin with?"

"How would that make sense?" Daniel asked, wrinkling his nose. "We followed it up to Lawn Lake. We saw the river mouth."

"But are you sure that's the river we got in?" Asher asked. "I remember seeing there was a glacier up on Rowe's peak. That means there has to be a ton of rivers and streams coming down from it. What if we went down one of those? We might be on the other side of the Mummy Range by now."

"Is that even possible?" Daniel asked, baffled. How could they end up on the other side of a mountain range without noticing?

"I don't know," Asher griped. "I'm just trying to think of an explanation that makes more sense than 'someone picked us up out of the Roaring River and dropped us in some totally different river miles away.'"

"This is insane." Daniel put his head in his hands, wanting nothing more than to be at home in his own bed. He didn't even care if he was alone anymore. He just didn't want to be out here a second longer.

"We should keep going," Asher said after a long, silent moment. "The sooner we get above the trees, the sooner we can figure out where we are."

Daniel resisted the urge, though it was a powerful one, to say something nasty about what an effective trail guide Asher had proven to be so far. Instead he just went on sitting a while longer, until he had his breath back and thought he could stand it again. Then he stood, helped Asher to his feet, and together they continued to limp on, further up the mountain.

Chapter Ten

They made frequent stops, on Daniel's insistence, his ankle in too much pain and his concern about how increasingly pale Asher was becoming too great to ignore. Thus it was past noon and edging towards evening as they reached an elevation high enough to get a better look around them. In thin-lipped silence, Asher stared at the wilderness that stretched around them. Daniel could see him desperately looking for something he recognized, and if the growing furrow between his brows was anything to go by, he wasn't finding it.

Daniel scanned for any sign of something man-made. A tower or a building—anything that would indicate the presence of people. There were only more mountains and forest in every direction. Daniel thought he saw water glittering somewhere in the distance, but he couldn't identify the river, and there were entirely too many mountains to tell them apart. The corners of Asher's mouth pulled down into something like a grimace.

"You don't know where we are, do you?" Daniel said, more tired than upset. "Why am I not surprised? You are the worst trail guide ever."

"I know where we are," Asher hissed through clenched teeth. "We must be near...Desolation Peak.

And that means. Um. That's Spruce Canyon. And if we keep going that way, we'll find Bridal Veil Falls."

Daniel eyed Asher critically, trying to remember if he had seen all those names on the map. He supposed he didn't have any option but just to believe the trail guide. After all, Daniel didn't have any better idea of where they should go. At least Asher was giving them a direction. Still, Daniel wished he could spot just one man-made structure. Just one building or trail or road to head towards. But everything just looked like wilderness in all directions.

"Okay," Daniel sighed. "So we head down that way? And we'll find Bridal Veil Falls?"

"Yeah," Asher sounded like he was trying to convince himself as much as Daniel. "Yeah definitely. And the falls are a huge attraction, so there will definitely be people there."

"That's all I needed to hear," Daniel laughed, only a little bitter, and secured his arm around Asher's shoulders again as the two men continued limping onwards, praying they were making the right decision.

"If we live through this," Daniel said as they picked their way carefully down a slope, "I'm quitting my job. It's not worth seeing Donahue's smug face every day. I work hard. I have a great resume. I could get a way better job. Probably better pay too. And a normal boss wouldn't force me to come on stupid camping trips or deal with accounting paperwork I am clearly not qualified for or—"

"He had you doing his accounting?" Asher asked, suddenly curious. "I totally support you ditching his ass, by the way."

"'Doing his accounting' implies he wanted me to actually look at the papers," Daniel said, rolling his eyes, "rather than just signing off and sending them to records. I told him the numbers were a mess and we needed a professional CPA, but he wouldn't listen to me. He never listens to me or anyone but his own utterly inane whims—"

"Yeah, he's a real piece of work," Asher interrupted again. "What was wrong with the accounting paperwork?"

"More like what wasn't wrong with it," Daniel griped, happy to vent and pleased Asher was letting him. "Unreported and unlabeled expenditures, money just appearing and disappearing willy-nilly or else going around in circles. He runs the business like his personal playground and expects all of us to just make it work somehow, when he won't even do his paperwork correctly. Working with him is a nightmare."

"Sounds like it," Asher sounded thoughtful, his eyes on the tree line ahead of them. "I've had a few bad bosses. But Donahue is in a class of his own."

"It's been worse since his father died," Daniel went on. "Even after he retired, Donahue Senior kept an eye on things and made sure they didn't get too out of hand. Donahue Junior has been running rampant since the day of his father's funeral."

They were beginning to be surrounded by trees again, and Daniel worried, observing their lopsided, limping gait, how they would manage to continue going in the right direction to find the falls. Not to mention, he was getting hungry. It had been almost a full day since the granola bar.

"So, Mr. Trail Guide," Daniel said after a moment. "Do you know if there's anything edible on this mountain?"

Asher breathed heavily through his nose again, something Daniel noticed he did every time Daniel asked him something he didn't want to answer. "Sure," he said. "There's, uh. Raspberries. And currants. Gooseberries."

"Its fall, though," Daniel interrupted. "I don't think there's going to be a lot of berries."

"Cacti, then," Asher tried. "Prickly pear."

"I think we're too high up for those?"

"Shit. Mushrooms, probably?"

Daniel stared at the other man in bewildered irritation.

"Don't they make you get some kind of certification before you can be a trail guide?" Daniel asked, beginning to run out of patience. "You had to take a class or something at least, right?"

"Well maybe I'm just not that great at studying, okay?" Asher snapped, uncomfortable.

"Then why did Donahue hire you?" Daniel pushed. "He's a lazy ass, but he always insists on the best. Why would he take you when you obviously don't know anything?"

"*Because I'm not a trail guide, damn it!*" Asher shouted, then winced in regret, holding his side. Daniel stared at him in bewildered anger, then abruptly dropped him, letting him fall against a nearby pine tree.

"I knew it!" Daniel shouted, as vindicated as he was offended. "I knew there was something not right about you! What are you then? Some drinking buddy of his? Are you his drug dealer? What? Tell me!"

"I'm his loan shark!" Asher answered, shoulders hunched defensively as he slid down the tree. "Fuck, I'm not even his loan shark. I work for his loan shark. Donahue owes big money to one of the local families. I came as their representative. He was supposed to pay me yesterday before the rafting trip, but he put me off, told me the money wasn't ready yet. He insisted he had to talk to the boss about some bullshit business venture. I was gonna break his kneecaps before the end of the trip, before this happened. I'm a thug, Daniel. Just a nothing thug. They just sent me because I look 'outdoorsy.'"

Daniel, stunned, stumbled back against a tree of his own—a stunted cottonwood—and slid slowly to the ground across from Asher.

"Holy shit," he mumbled. "You're a mob enforcer."

"That's technically a word for it I guess, but that makes me sound more important than I am..."

"That explains the tattoos."

"Hey!"

"You have no idea where we are, do you?"

He fixed Asher with an accusatory glare, and Asher looked away, shame clear in his expression. He didn't need to answer.

"You just read the same brochures I did," Daniel scoffed, hopes crumbling. "We just wandered into the wilderness on your direction, you idiot!"

"What else were we supposed to do?" Asher glared back, responding to Daniel's hostility in kind. "Just sit at the bottom of that ravine? At least I gave us something to do! Better than just waiting to die!"

"We were waiting to be rescued!" Daniel refused to back down. Angry, hopeless tears tried their best to overwhelm him though he pushed them down. "If we had just stayed where we were—"

"You mean with the bear?" Asher pointed out, sneering. "By the river no one knew we'd be on?"

"It was something." Daniel threw a handful of pine needles at Asher in irritation. "At least we weren't in the middle of nowhere without even a landmark!"

"It's a damn park!" Asher shouted, throwing a pine cone back at Daniel. "I figured if we kept walking we'd have to find a trail eventually!"

"Did you even look at the map?" Daniel screeched, batting the pine cone out of the air and throwing it and two more back, one of which hit Asher squarely in the head. "This park is bordered by wilderness on nearly every side! We could be walking out of the national park entirely for all you know, you useless, lying, homophobic, asshole—"

He was cut off as Asher, clearly tired of being hit with pine cones, threw himself across the little space between them with the apparent intent of strangling Daniel. They rolled in the pine needles, scuffling and scratching at each other for a moment, neither doing much damage except to themselves, agitating their own injuries. It was Asher who finally stopped, dropping onto Daniel's chest with an exhausted wheeze.

"I give, I give," he said, though he was lying on top of the smaller man. "That was stupid."

"Yeah, very," Daniel spat, dropping a handful of pine needles into the other man's hair spitefully before he flopped back onto the ground to wallow in the pain he'd caused himself.

"I'm sorry," Asher said after a moment, his head still pillowed on Daniel's chest. "I wasn't trying to get us even more lost. I should have said something earlier. I'm sorry."

Daniel let the apology stand for a moment, caught off guard by the sincerity of it. He hadn't expected such a thing from Asher. Especially not now that he knew what the man was. He supposed that made the confession all the more meaningful.

"I'm sorry I called you useless," Daniel replied, tense but trying to make peace. "And hit you with a pine cone."

They lay in silence for a moment, Asher's head rising with Daniel's breathing while they recovered. Daniel was too tired and in too much pain to care about the awkward position. They'd spooned last night and spent most of today hanging on to one another like human crutches. He'd just sort of accepted that Asher was going to be in his personal space from now on. Which was strange, he realized. He'd never even liked his previous girlfriends hanging on him that much. Was it just because of the situation they were in that he could tolerate Asher so well?

"And I'm not homophobic."

Daniel was distracted from his thoughts by the comment Asher grumbled into his sternum.

"You sure acted like it," Daniel pointed out, not willing to let him go easy on that one. "I would have punched you if I didn't think you'd kick my ass."

"I tried to tell you before the raft went over." Asher was still speaking into Daniel's shirt, not meeting his eye. "I'm gay."

"What?"

Daniel stared, uncomprehending, at the man lying on him, golden blonde hair full of pine needles. He must have misheard.

Asher lifted his head to look at Daniel so there was no chance his words would be muffled by torso. "I'm gay."

"Are mob enforcers allowed to be gay?"

"Christ man, it's 2016. Do you really think they care?"

Daniel let his head drop to the forest floor again, considering. "Then why all the insults?" Daniel asked, nose wrinkling in confusion. "Is it some kind of internalized self-hate thing?"

"What? No! I was...you know..." Asher shrugged, looking away, and cleared his throat. "I was flirting."

"Seriously?" Daniel scoffed, sitting up on his hands, forcing Asher to move as well. "That's how you flirt? Has anyone ever actually responded positively to that?"

Asher shrugged again, trying to find a comfortable position that didn't inflame the wound in his side. "It's not my normal game," he agreed. "But you were so easy to fluster, and so in denial... I got carried away. You're adorable when you blush."

Daniel, to his own consternation, blushed. "Well you can forget it," Daniel said sternly. "In case I didn't make it clear before, I'm straight."

"As a San Francisco road."

"I'm serious!" Daniel's voice rose again and he struggled to bring his temper back under control. "At least show me the respect of assuming I know my own sexuality, alright?"

Asher looked a little ashamed by that and leaned away, holding up his hands for peace.

"You're right. Sorry," he said, "Don't worry about it. It was just a passing thing anyway. You have a cute face but your personality is awful."

"Wow, thanks."

"You threw pine cones at me."

For some reason that just made Daniel laugh. He sat there for a moment, just laughing, until he could wipe the tears of mirth from his eyes and stand, helping Asher up after him.

"Let's just keep moving," he decided. "We won't get found just waiting here so far from where we landed. So we might as well try and find a trail. There was some kind of body of water this way. And where there's water there's usually people."

"Good plan," Asher agreed with a nod. Holding each other up like nothing had happened, the two men limped forward, both hoping they were going the right way, doing their best not to think about the dire situation they were in.

Chapter Eleven

The forest grew denser as they trudged downhill, the underbrush soon becoming tangled and thorny and difficult to walk through, slowing their already slow progress significantly. And the sun was beginning to set as well. Daniel's stomach growled painfully. More than once they had to stop going forward and pick their way around small, sheer drops and banks too steep to drop over in their condition. Daniel felt like he'd been through hell and back and he wanted nothing so much as a good night's sleep in a comfortable bed. Instead, as it grew dark, they stopped at the base of one of those banks and gathered branches for another hastily assembled lean-to.

"Should we try to make a fire?" Daniel asked as they settled down under the scant covering of a few loose tree branches. They were lashed together with a vine Daniel really hoped wasn't poison ivy and lined with the foil blanket.

"I don't know how," Asher confessed. "Not without a starter. I tried to learn that two sticks thing in Cub Scouts. Frickin' impossible."

"Yeah, I don't know how to do that either," Daniel confessed, unrolling the sleeping bag. "And it feels like it's going to be cold tonight."

The temperature was dropping fast, frost already appearing on the edges of things. It was going to be a rough night without a fire. He eyed the sleeping bag.

"Looks like it's going to be another night of cuddling," Asher grinned at Daniel and, now that he wasn't mistaking it for mocking, Daniel could tell the man wasn't faking his happiness about that. At least one of them was getting some enjoyment out of this nightmare.

"At least it'll be fully clothed this time," Daniel sighed.

It was already almost too dark to see. Daniel peered around their improvised campsite, wary of bugs and snakes and wishing the neon sign of a burger joint would appear out of the darkness. He'd walk another half mile in the dark for a cheeseburger right now.

Instead he used the last of the light to check on Asher's wound, frowning as he saw it was still bleeding sluggishly through the soaked bandages. It was never going to close if Asher didn't get some rest. And Asher would only get weaker in the meantime. But they couldn't afford to just stop. He didn't say anything and Asher didn't ask. Instead he opened the sleeping bag and both men climbed in, glad it was wide enough to fit them both, even if it was a tight squeeze. Daniel did his best to zip the bag around them and keep in the warmth.

It had been an exhausting day, and Daniel expected that sleep would have to come easily. Instead it eluded him. He lay awake, terribly conscious of Asher's chest pressed against his back. The other man had fallen asleep almost at once, his arm around Daniel like a beloved teddy bear. Daniel pondered why he had to be the little spoon again. At least this time there was more than just thin underwear between his backside and Asher's hips. Especially with the way Asher kept shifting in his sleep, rocking his hips against Daniel in a way that Daniel almost suspected intentional. But Asher was definitely asleep. Daniel could feel the other man's warm, shallow breaths stirring the hair at the nape of his neck.

He closed his eyes tightly and forced his heart to slow, wondering why he was acting like a hormonal teenager, now of all times. It wasn't like he'd never slept next to a woman this way. But somehow it had never felt this intimate before, never agitated him to the point of sleeplessness. Maybe Asher was right, he thought, stomach twisting. Maybe he was in denial? He shoved that thought away quickly and hunkered down further into the bag, determined to sleep. There was no way he was gay. Asher was just projecting, and Daniel was only considering it because of the stressful situation they were in. Once this was over, he would go back to his normal life and never consider something like that again.

He did eventually sleep, and his dreams were strange, conflicted things. He was in the river again, but this time the figure on the other side was reaching through, pulling him out. He looked at it and saw his own face, dead, frozen solid. He slung his frozen corpse onto his back and walked, carrying it, back into the city and up to his office. He worked, ignoring the rictus grin of the body that wore his face and hung near his ear all day. He laid it in his bed at night and it talked, telling him awful things. The kind of things his parents had never said out loud, but that he'd always suspected they felt. The kind of things he himself had thought and been too ashamed to ever admit. When it was done, he turned out the light, went into the bathroom, and climbed through the mirror to take his place on the other side. As he plunged through its silver surface, he found himself in the river again, once more desperately stretching for air. But there were arms around him, warm and tight, dragging him down into the deep dark waters. And as they squeezed him closer, he stopped caring whether he reached the surface again. It was fine down here where he was wanted.

He woke in the morning shivering, his head throbbing with hunger. He felt even worse than he had yesterday, and no amount of snuggling from Asher, who seemed to be under the impression that Daniel was his personal stuffed toy, could correct it. No wonder he'd had so many dreams about being clung to. The man was an octopus. Daniel practically had to scrape him off with a spatula.

Daniel struggled out of the sleeping bag in silence and the two men began cleaning up their little camp, such as it was, sharing the last of the water and storing the sleeping bag and thermal blanket again. Daniel felt weak and distracted from hunger and every part of his body was in varying degrees of pain. He'd reached the point where he didn't know how to process it anymore. The pain just was, and it was endless. He and Asher limped on, silent in the early morning mist, too tired and stiff and hungry and cold to speak to one another.

Daniel scanned the underbrush ceaselessly for a sign of anything remotely edible. He was going to be ready to start stuffing leaves into his mouth at random soon. How long could a person live without food before starving? Especially while doing something as calorie intensive as hiking all day while injured? He had a feeling it wasn't long. They needed to find somewhere sheltered to hide before they ran out of energy. If they could rest and conserve their strength, maybe they could catch something. A rabbit maybe. Thinking of rabbit was a mistake. Daniel pushed the thought away as his hunger clawed at him.

Hunger made him sullen, and as the sun rose and the day got no warmer, his temper only worsened. Judging by Asher's icy glare, it wasn't doing great things for his mood either. They just needed to catch a break, Daniel thought. Just a little luck to keep them going.

They both saw the bird at the same time. A fat grouse, speckled brown with a white and red spot on its neck. The two men froze, both considering what their chances of catching it might be. They weren't even thinking about how they would cook it. As long as they could catch it, that was all that mattered. Asher caught Daniel's eye and, with a slow nod, began to circle as quietly as possible around the bird. Daniel went in the other direction, ready to catch it if it ran towards him, or else drive it back towards Asher. Daniel's heart was hammering, his mouth watering already, imagining grouse must not be too different from chicken. He couldn't wait to be full again. It would make walking so much easier, even on his sprained—

His sprained ankle, already complaining loudly from the ceaseless walking, buckled. Daniel caught himself, but not before he'd stumbled, the noise startling the grouse, which took to the air. Asher jumped after it, only to stop short with a wheeze of pain as the movement stretched his injury. They both took a moment to regain their breath and let what had just happened sink in before Asher kicked at a bush, cursing loudly.

"Son of a bitch!" he swore, abusing the bush some more. "Why the hell did you make that noise? We almost had it!"

"I tripped, alright?" Daniel, defensive, glared back at Asher in defiance. "Why didn't you catch it? It flew right towards you!"

"Because I have a damn hole in my side!" Asher shot back. "You're the one who should have been catching it!"

"I wouldn't have had to catch it if you hadn't spooked that bear and made us lose all our supplies!"

"Spooked it? What the hell else was I supposed to do? It was about to eat you!"

"No, it wasn't! Not until you made it think we were a threat by yelling and running. If you were a real trail guide you would have known that."

"And we're back to this again." Asher threw his hands in the air and turned away, stomping off in the direction they'd been walking before they'd seen the grouse. "I said I was sorry, okay?"

"Sorry doesn't really cut it when we're starving to death in the middle of nowhere." Daniel limped after the other man, glad for the anger if only because it distracted him from how hungry he was.

"I tell you what," Asher laughed bitterly. "If I die first, you're cordially invited to *eat my fucking ass*!"

Clinging to their anger to fuel them, the two men stomped onwards in silence, glaring and exchanging furious insults whenever they began to lose steam. By afternoon, Daniel's head was throbbing, his pulse pounding painfully in his ears, his throat raw from yelling at his companion. Asher was pale as a ghost and moving even slower than Daniel's limping pace, clearly not going to make it much farther. Daniel didn't think he would be far behind the other man. His muscles burned from prolonged exertion with nothing to refuel them. He felt dizzy, and he'd stopped caring about walking any further. He just wanted to lie down and go to sleep.

They found a small stream and paused to refill the water bottle and drink to fill their empty stomachs. Daniel contemplated whether they could catch any of the minnows darting in the shallow water. He had a feeling that even if he did, they wouldn't go far enough to be worth it. "Do you think this stream leads to the lake we saw yesterday?" he asked.

"How should I know?" Asher bared his teeth, too exhausted to look threatening. "I'm not a real trail guide, remember?"

"We should follow it," Daniel didn't have the energy to argue. "It's better than wandering blind, and at least we won't run out of water."

"Whatever." was Asher's only answer. They carried on walking beside the narrow stream, Daniel hoping it would somehow lead them to a five-star hotel and a free steak dinner. Or even a truck stop and a microwave burrito. He wasn't picky anymore. He just wanted to be somewhere comfortable with food.

He kept thinking of his sparse little apartment, how bare and empty it was. Nothing unnecessary or complicated. Barely even anything decorative. And he always ate the same things and never really enjoyed them. If he got out of here, he was going to turn his apartment into a comfortable, pleasant place to be. No more of the empty uneasiness that kept him at work late so that he wouldn't have to face being alone. He'd fill his home with pillows and colorful decorations and teach himself to be less gloomy and antisocial somehow. And he'd never eat anything he didn't love, or hold back from indulging in things that made him happy. If he made it through this, he was going to start a new life.

"Asher," he said, stumbling a little on the loose stone bank of the stream, his ankle throbbing dully. Everything was dull now. "If we get out of this, what will you do?"

"Don't if me," Asher snorted, his breath a fog of derision riding the air before him. He split it as he passed through it. "We're going to be fine. It's only been two days."

"You didn't answer the question."

Asher made an irritated sound in the back of his throat. "First I'm going to murder your boss," he replied with deadly seriousness. "Then I'm going to sleep for a week. And then I'll just go back to how I've always been. What, are you planning some big life change because you almost died?"

He looked back at Asher and the scorn in his eyes scalded Daniel worse than the cold air.

"Sorry to disappoint you," Asher went on, "but this is just a shitty weekend for me. I'll forget about it in a year."

Daniel felt spite rising in him again, and it didn't matter whether Asher was just doing it to keep himself moving or not. Daniel didn't want the other man looking at him with that disdain.

"Of course you will," Daniel spat back like acid. "Because everything is a joke to you, right? If you never take anything seriously then it can never really affect you, is that it? Well guess what, you might be great at shutting off your emotions and pretending everything is just funny, but not everyone wants to be an emotionally stunted child for the rest of their lives. You don't get to just insult people and claim they can't take a joke when they get angry. You can't just ignore nearly dying with someone. You don't get to dismiss this, asshole!"

"I'll dismiss whatever I damn well please!" Asher didn't even stop, just hunching his shoulders as Daniel moved closer, like he was walking against the wind. "Maybe I joke too much, but at least I try to act like a human being and not a damn robot! You sit off by yourself, hissing at anyone who gets too close, then have the audacity to look lonely. I hide my feelings, sure, but you try to pretend like you never had them at all! You're just as stunted as I am. At least I can admit to myself how I'm feeling. You're still deluding yourself into thinking you're straight."

"I told you to give that up!" Daniel wanted to scream with frustration. "I'm not gay! Just because you have some kind of crush on me—"

"I do *not* have a crush on you," Asher stopped then, turning to snarl in Daniel's face. "I thought you were cute for about half a minute. You've done a very thorough job of proving me wrong."

"Then why do you keep trying to force this on me?" Daniel, unintimidated, got right back in the other man's face. "If you're not still trying to convince me to sleep with you, why do you care so much whether I'm gay or not?"

"Because I feel bad for you, dumbass!" Asher shouted back, then stumbled. He was white as a sheet, the exertion clearly beginning to get to him. Daniel caught him reflexively, ready to drop the argument so the weakened man could sit down, but Asher kept going.

"Do you think I haven't been right where you are?" Asher asked, voice losing its vehemence as his energy drained. "Ignoring my feelings, desperately denying everything I felt, scared shitless that someone was going to notice I wasn't normal? Only I had a damn good reason for needing to hide. You have nothing holding you back and you're still torturing yourself! Can you blame me for wanting to save you?"

His voice dwindled further, his eyes trying to close. Daniel was holding the other man up completely now, his ankle screaming in protest.

"Hey. Hey! Pull it together!" Daniel demanded. "Don't pass out here! Come on!"

But Asher was already gone. Daniel had no choice but to lower the man to the ground as gently as possible and resign himself to making camp early. It was still early afternoon, but he supposed neither of them really had the energy to keep going. He laid Asher down with his head on the rolled up sleeping bag, then got to work making their shelter for the night, stopping whenever his ankle forced him to in order to rest and check on Asher. The man's clothes were soaked through with blood. He must have been in an absurd amount of pain, but he'd kept going anyway. It forced Daniel to keep going too, out of spite if nothing else.

Daniel had been so close to giving up. Had Asher been able to tell? Daniel felt a creeping sense of shame as he built a rough lean-to from fallen fir branches around the unconscious man and lined it with the space blanket. Then he spent the last of the light lying on the bank of the stream, catching as many minnows as he could with his hands. They might not go far, but anything was better than nothing. He took a crack at trying to start a fire and wished he had

109

his reading glasses. It would have made this much easier. As it was, all he did was give himself a blister rubbing sticks together.

The sun began to sink below the mountains and the forest only got colder. He watched white frost creep over the edges of red leaves and shivered. Loose skins of ice twirled across the surface of the river as it froze unevenly, not yet cold enough to catch the moving water. Daniel had a brief, impulsive thought of just throwing himself in and letting the numb cold ease his pain. He pushed that thought away fast. It had only been two days. They could still survive this.

His breath was a ghost, white and delicate as a cobweb, which coiled over the surface of the stream. He shivered, his hands wet and blue with cold. Daniel had thought it was supposed to get warmer as they moved down into the valley. Had they ended up going uphill anyway? He wouldn't be surprised if it was true. Both of them were hopelessly out of their depth. He sat watching the sun vanish behind the trees, his breath fogging before him, and waited for Asher to wake up.

The forest was eerie in the sunset, the light drenching the trees in red and gold. Animal noises diminished to almost nothing and left the world in eerie silence except for the rustle of the wind through the leaves. Pine needles waving were a subtler, more distinct sound from that of deciduous leaves, which tended to sound like rolling surf. This was quieter, more like the shuffle of fabric. The hem of a dress across the floor in the middle of the night. The rising of curtains on an empty stage.

Daniel wondered if Asher would wake up at all. Maybe he'd pushed too hard, lost too much blood. Maybe Daniel was alone out here now. His heart beat sped up at the thought and he shifted closer to Asher, checking to make sure the other man was still breathing. He took Asher's hand, just to soothe himself, squeezing it as he watched the forest darken around them like something from a horror film. Red light filtered like fingers through the black branches, reaching for him with sinister purpose. He closed his eyes, trying to block out the fear rising in him. He couldn't be alone out here. He wouldn't be able to take it. He squeezed Asher's hand tighter and willed the man to wake up.

"You trying to crush me, kid?"

Daniel opened his eyes, relief flooding him, and saw Asher looking up at him. The other man looked more tired than Daniel had ever seen anyone look. He looked like he was dying. His face was as white as Daniel's breath and his grip was weak and cold.

"I know I pissed you off, but I don't think breaking my hand is called for," Asher raised his eyebrows and Daniel released the other man's hand at once, amazed he could still try to be funny when he looked close to death.

"I thought you were gone for a minute there," Daniel confessed, too scared to be dishonest, his voice a thin whisper. "I thought I was alone."

Asher seemed to sense the genuine distress in Daniel's voice and for once didn't tease him. Instead he took Daniel's hand again, squeezing it with all the little strength he had left. "It's okay, Carter," the other man said. "I don't want to be alone out here either."

"I'm afraid of the dark," Daniel's skin crawled with shame, but it was obvious enough already that he was. "My parents—they used to lock me in my room when I misbehaved, like any kid. But I hated it. I hated being alone so much. I'd cry and hammer on the door. And then one time, at night, the lightbulb in my room went out while I was locked in. I remember seeing a light reflected in the mirror on the wall and being sure there was someone in there with me. My parents thought all the yelling was just me wanting out like normal. Didn't unlock the door for hours. They apologized after, but…"

The story spilled out of Daniel like water from his lips, like the spectral clouds of his breath, surprising him as much as he was sure it surprised Asher. He was shaking, and holding Asher's hand tightly. Thinking he was alone had really spooked him for a minute.

"It's okay," Asher said again. "I'm not going anywhere. We're in this together."

It wasn't like Daniel had forgotten he was angry at Asher. The anger was still there. Just less important at the moment. Asher made the arguments easy to forget.

"I got us food," Daniel said. "Sort of."

He pulled over the palm fan covered in raw minnows.

"Gross," Asher observed lightly. "But better than nothing."

They split Daniel's little catch as the last of the light vanished. Not being able to see the minnows did not make eating them easier. At least they could mostly be swallowed without needing to be chewed. They hardly put a dent in Daniel's hunger, but he knew Asher was right. Anything was better than nothing.

When they were done, they climbed into the sleeping bag, but even within it, Daniel could feel the growing cold. He shivered, and for once let Asher cuddle close to him without complaint. They were going to get out of this, he reminded himself. This wasn't the end. Even if he could smell Asher's blood on the night air.

Chapter Twelve

He woke to Asher shaking him and knew he'd only been asleep a few hours. It was pitch dark. He felt sluggish and numb.

"Get up," Asher hissed, "Get up. We need to move."

Daniel groaned, trying to ignore the other man, but Asher kept shaking him. Daniel finally complied, stumbling out of the lean-to. It was only then he realized he wasn't in any pain. He could hardly feel any of his injuries at all. As Asher hounded him, making him walk in circles, Daniel began to realize just how cold he was, teeth chattering violently. The fog over his mind began to clear. It was snowing, he realized, and hard, the wind howling and whipping powder into their paltry little shelter. They had nearly frozen. If Asher hadn't woken them up...

"We can't stay here," Asher said. "We have to move. If we lay down again, we'll die."

Daniel nodded numbly, and together they grabbed the sleeping bag and blanket. Asher put the space blanket around Daniel's shoulders and wore the sleeping bag around his own as the two men stumbled downstream, following the little creek towards anything and nothing, just afraid to stop moving.

The numbness that was making walking on his ankle bearable again quickly wore off, and Daniel felt even worse for having been at least moderately pain free for a moment there. He didn't know if it was a good sign or a bad one that he could feel his injuries again.

The snow fell harder and heavier, as though offended that they had escaped its killing them in their sleep. Between it and the darkness, Daniel could barely see. They just pressed forward, finding the creek again when they nearly stepped in it a dozen times. Asher trudged with his head down, just moving to keep moving, but Daniel couldn't help watching the dark world around them—the blue black sky obscured by white, the moon a blinding traitor, lost in the powder. Branches creaked in the high wind and bent under the weight of gathering snow. Daniel kept a hand bunched in Asher's shirt, terrified of losing the other man in the white out. He was so cold, and he kept stumbling. He couldn't keep walking much longer.

And then, for a moment, the trees cleared, and Daniel saw something that was too big to be a tree and too regular to be a rock. He tried to call Asher's name, but the noise of the wind was too loud. Instead he just dragged on Asher's arm until the other man realized what Daniel was pointing at. They stumbled towards the shape in the darkness together.

Daniel sobbed with relief when he felt wood under his hands. Proper, processed logs, not a tree. He fumbled and soon found a door. Together, he and Asher fell through into a dark, still cabin.

Some small rodent scrambled away as they crashed in, slamming the door behind them. The room was not large, but it was indoors and insulated from the cold and Daniel didn't need much else. Peering around the room by the faint snow light coming through the window, Daniel noticed there was a cot in one corner, and a rudimentary kitchen with a wood burning stove, moldering firewood still stacked beside it.

"It's a ranger station," Asher said as Daniel went to collapse on the cot. "It looks abandoned. But there must have been a trail through here at some point."

"It has a roof and a bed," Daniel sighed.

"Better than that," Asher gave a bark of laughter. "Even when they abandon these places, they leave supplies behind, in case of emergencies."

He was digging through the dusty, cobwebbed cabinets. Daniel tried to will himself to get up and help, but he couldn't convince himself to move. At last Asher stumbled towards the cot, only to kneel and look under it. He whooped with delight and pulled out a metal locker, opening it.

Daniel watched with wonder as Asher revealed blankets, fresh clothes, MREs—everything they needed to survive. Daniel cheered as well, elation momentarily banishing his exhaustion. Laughing with unhinged delight, the two men threw their arms around each other in an exultant embrace. They both tore into a pack of dehydrated food and wrapped new blankets around their shoulders and sat with their backs against the bed, relishing the relative warmth from the storm. Cold spaghetti had never been so delicious. There were flameless ration heaters in the MREs, but neither Daniel nor Asher had the patience to use them right now. They spoke little as they ate, their mouths too full, but as they grinned at each other over their food it was clear all was forgiven. Both of them were just happy the other was alive.

Once Asher had eaten enough to stop shaking, he took the matches and starter blocks from the supplies and set about starting a fire in the stove. The house was vastly better than being outside, but it was still cold enough for their breath to be visible. Fortunately, even if Cub Scouts hadn't taught Asher how to make a fire from nothing, it had taught him how to build one from something, and although the firewood was old it burned well. Soon the tiny cabin was filling with heat, and Daniel let the extra blanket slip off, sighing with relief. As he relaxed, he noticed a first aid kit in the supplies. He opened it, flipping through its contents to make sure they weren't too degraded by time.

"Asher," he said when he saw they weren't. "Come here. We can finally do something about that hole in your side."

Asher looked wary, but they moved in front of the fire and the larger man lifted up his shirt to reveal the stiff, soaked bandages. Daniel grimaced, but got to work cutting them away so that he could see the actual injury.

"The good news is," he said as he cleaned it with alcohol and water, "it doesn't look infected. And the bleeding definitely isn't as bad as it was that first day. I think you'll be okay. We should probably still try and stitch it, since we don't know how much longer we'll be out here."

Asher took a deep breath, looking supremely unenthused about that idea.

"I don't suppose there's any anesthetic in that box?" Asher asked with a nervous laugh.

Daniel leaned over to lift out a bottle of whiskey.

"That'll work."

Asher took two shots, Daniel took one, and then he threaded a suture needle and got to work, grateful the hole was small. Two or three stitches would likely be enough. Knowing that didn't make it any less gross for Daniel or any less painful for Asher. But Daniel got it done.

"Before I re-bandage this," he said, glancing up from spreading disinfectant gel. "Do you want to wash—?"

He paused, caught off guard as he realized Asher was staring down at him with unexpected intensity, the firelight reflected in those startlingly blue eyes.

"Probably a good idea," Asher agreed, not breaking his stare. "But moving is kind of difficult right now. Plus, my clothes."

Asher's clothes on that side were stiff with blood.

"There was some spare sweaters and things in the emergency supplies," Daniel suggested, tearing his eyes away from that stare, unsure why it made him so uncomfortable. "They'll do until we can wash your stuff."

"Fair enough," Asher agreed, and began taking off his clothing without another word.

Daniel helped him, despite his embarrassment, knowing the other man's range of motion was limited right now. When he was down to his underwear, Daniel soaked a cloth in water. "Just relax," he said. "I've got this."

Asher didn't argue, lying still as Daniel leaned over him, gently wiping away the dried blood and accumulated grime of several days hiking. Daniel tried not to acknowledge the intimacy of what he was doing, even as he was dragging the damp wash cloth down the taut muscle of Asher's thighs, the moisture glistening on his tanned skin in the glow of the fire.

They were just taking care of each other. Keeping each other alive, the same way they had been since Asher had pulled him out of the river. He would have done this for anyone. But part of him knew that, for anyone else, his heart would not be racing like this, his touch lingering on Asher's chest, tracing the patterns of his tattoos.

"I don't think there's any blood up there Danny," Asher pointed out, and Daniel pulled away, cursing how quick he was to blush.

"Just being thorough," he said, telling himself he believed it. "That should be enough. Sit up and I'll bandage it."

Asher did as he was told, still watching Daniel with those intense eyes, while Daniel quickly wrapped the bandage around Asher's waist. When it was done, he started packing up the first aid kit again busily.

"Hopefully, that'll hold you until we can get back to civilization," Daniel said, not meeting Asher's eye. "Try not to move too much. I've never stitched anything before and I don't know how secure those are."

"They're fine," Asher assured him. "I've been stitched up more than once. I can tell."

Daniel smiled, appreciating the vote of confidence, but as Daniel moved to stand and put the first aid kit away, Asher caught his sleeve. Daniel looked down at him, catching that blue gaze.

"Don't you want to get cleaned up too?" he asked.

Daniel swallowed hard, realizing he was falling into something dangerous.

"There's only one bed here," Asher said with a grin. "I'd rather share it with someone clean. No offense."

He had a point. Daniel looked away, considering it for a moment. "Fine." he said, "Just put away the supplies, would you?"

Asher nodded and turned to repack everything they had dragged out while Daniel pulled off his clothing. He'd slept naked with the man before, but for some reason it was only now he couldn't stop casting self-conscious glances in Asher's direction. He set his clothes aside and soaked the wash cloth again, sitting close to the fire as he cleaned himself. It was a relief to clear away all the dirt and grime, especially from the host of cuts and abrasions he'd acquired in the tumble down the river and over the cliff. His ankle and shoulder looked the worst—his ankle swollen and angry from being walked on, his shoulder still one big purple bruise. He ran the washcloth over his shoulder, feeling the water run down his back, and winced at even the slight pressure on it.

"Hey."

Asher's voice, unexpectedly close, spooked Daniel and made him drop the washcloth. Asher, sitting just behind him, picked it up, offering Daniel an ace bandage with his other hand.

"I found it while I was packing everything else up," he said. "For your ankle. You can't be treating my injuries and ignoring your own."

"Right, thanks," Daniel agreed, embarrassed, and accepted the bandage, leaning down to begin wrapping it around his ankle. He wasn't sure if it would do much good with how much he'd already walked on it, but he supposed it had to be better than nothing.

He'd barely begun when he was startled again by the touch of a wet washcloth against his back. He looked back at Asher for an explanation, but the man only smiled.

"You don't need to do that," Daniel protested. "You should be resting."

"You took care of me," Asher replied with a shrug. "I should return the favor. Besides, doing this much won't hurt me."

He seemed determined, running the cloth over Daniel's shoulders. Daniel, uneasy, let him continue, returning to bandaging his foot. The rough terrycloth was soothing against his skin even if the water was cold, running down his back in rivulets that gathered on the floor beneath him.

Asher was patient and thorough, taking his time as the cloth drifted lower over Daniel's ribs, towards the small of his back. Daniel, done with his ankle, felt his heart skip a beat as Asher leaned closer. He felt the cloth on his hip and Asher's other hand on his arm as the larger man pressed a single warm kiss to the back of Daniel's neck.

"All done," Asher reported in a low, satisfied tone, pulling away and leaving Daniel feeling cold for more than one reason. He said nothing about the kiss, and neither did Daniel.

Daniel hurried to put his clothes back on, heart racing. Behind him Asher was pulling on long thermal underwear and a sweater from the box. They didn't fit well, but they were better than nothing. Daniel felt better and more civilized than he had since the river.

"Well, now that we're clean and fed," Asher said, hoisting the bottle of whiskey. "How about we enjoy ourselves a little before bed?"

The wiser part of Daniel knew this was, without question, a bad idea, but he nodded anyway, smiling. "Just a little though," he argued. "We don't need hangovers in the morning on top of everything else."

Asher laughed. "The day I get hung over from one bottle of whiskey is the day I give up drinking," he said, and poured a shot into the cap.

Chapter Thirteen

As the wiser part of Daniel had warned him would happen, more than half the whiskey bottle was soon gone, and the two men, well beyond tipsy though not truly blind drunk, were leaning on each other, laughing hysterically at some anecdote Asher was struggling to finish.

"So then the guy...He's still insisting he can pay, right?" Asher wheezed between laughing. "And he just keeps coming back with more goats! Until there's just a herd of them out in front of the building, and every time the machine inside goes off they all fall over like a ton of bowling pins. Like thirty of these tiny goats just lying all over the place and this crazy yokel standing in the middle and demanding we take them!"

Daniel was laughing so hard he could barely breathe, clinging to Asher to keep himself upright, tears of mirth in his eyes. "God," he said when he could speak again, gulping for air. "I had no idea the life of a mob thug was actually a sitcom."

"Well, I'm sugar coating a lot, obviously," Asher was still chuckling, leaning back against the bed as he tried to recover. "But honestly, that's what it feels like some days. People will do the most absurd bullshit when they think they're beyond the law. Not even illegal shit, just *weird* shit. I could get three degrees in psychology and I probably still wouldn't understand it. People are a fuckin' mystery."

"Agreed," Daniel chuckled. "Just the people in my office are so baffling sometimes. Like Lynda. I don't think I've ever actually learned her last name because she's so insistent on everyone calling her Lynda. With a Y! And what's with all the cacti? She fusses over them like they're priceless orchids or something. I thought the whole point of succulents is that you don't have to take care of them?"

"You're one to talk," Asher laughed. "You're the most baffling person I ever met. Do you have any idea how confusing you are? At first I thought all that stuck up stiffness was because you thought you were too good for everyone. Then it turns out it's actually the opposite, and you're just screamingly insecure and can't open up about it—"

"Hey," Daniel frowned, in too good a mood to be properly insulted but not wanting to let it go either. Asher grinned and held up his hands apologetically.

"You look like this soft, delicate thing," Asher went on, "but out here you've been tougher than pretty much anyone I've ever met. You're brave as hell. You pulled that stick out of me with barely a complaint, kept my dumb ass alive all this time. And then you tell me you're scared of the dark. People are confusing but you—you're something special."

For some reason, that made Daniel smile. Asher thought he was special. He was slumped against the other man's side, grinning up at him. The whiskey felt warm inside him, and he was still flush with relief at their survival. Outside a blizzard was raging that would have certainly killed them if they'd remained out in it, and instead they'd found this place and were in better shape than they had been since getting lost. The little bit of luck Daniel had been praying for had showed up after all. And right now, safe and warm and full, Asher looking down at him with those powerful blue eyes while the wind howled outside the walls and the fire cast golden shadows on his face, Daniel couldn't think of anywhere else he would rather be.

And then Asher kissed him.

It happened so slowly and naturally that Daniel almost didn't realize what was happening. Asher's mouth was warm against his, and though his lips were chapped from the cold and his chin was stubbled from days without shaving, it was the sweetest kiss Daniel had ever experienced. There was no urgency to it. Asher was in no rush. It just was, and it was perfect. Daniel could taste the whiskey on Asher's lips, and the graze of his tongue sent shivers up Daniel's spine like a rush of electricity. He'd kissed women before, plenty of times. Even, maybe especially, while drunk like this. He couldn't blame it on the drink or the situation or Asher's skill. And yet he knew no kiss had ever been this good before. Heat pooled like honey, dripping lower.

And then it was over. Asher broke the kiss to breathe, meeting Daniel's eyes. Daniel could see the worry in his gaze, afraid he'd done the wrong thing. Daniel felt like his emotions were on a roulette wheel, spinning through his head at full speed, no one knowing what they would land on. Should he be angry? Ashamed and embarrassed? Excited?

The roulette spun to a stop on none of those things. Instead, Daniel just smiled, awkward and sad, and slowly pulled away.

"Good night, Asher," he said, the finality unquestionable. He fixed the blankets on the cot and lay down, his face to the wall. Asher said nothing, and for a moment there was only silence. Daniel heard the clink of the whiskey bottle as the tattooed man took another shot. Then the bed creaked as he climbed in. He didn't try anything. He didn't even put his arm around Daniel the way he usually did, giving Daniel his space for once. Daniel appreciated it at least as much as he regretted it. They fell asleep quickly, aided by drink and exhaustion, close together and yet worlds apart on the tiny cot.

Daniel woke first in the morning and stirred up the fire again, tearing into one of the MREs and heating up the coffee he found inside. He limped to the window as he drank it, and saw the snow still falling lightly outside.

"We should probably stay another day," Asher said behind him, holding his own coffee. "Rest and recover while we can. I think there was a map in the supplies. We can plan our way home."

"Sounds like a plan," Daniel agreed.

The snow outside wasn't bad, so after a little while Daniel took the dirty clothes out to the stream. He broke the thin sheet of ice that had sealed the shallow water, then scrubbed the blood out of Asher's shirt against the rocks.

The morning was quiet. A crow cawed somewhere in the trees. The early snow blanketed the world in soft white, against which the black branches of pine were all the starker. Like the dark bones of the world pressing through skin. The stream ran through it, motion frozen, a glittering blue vein, dead to all eyes but still pumping just below the cold surface.

Daniel and Asher had so far exchanged only a few cordial words. The tension between them lay as still and unbroken as the ice on the stream, glittering in the sunlight that would soon melt it. Daniel wasn't certain their problems could be resolved so easily into dew. The kiss had changed things.

For all his assertions that he didn't want Daniel that way, when Asher had kissed him, Daniel had seen the desire in his eyes, and he had seen that it was not just lust. If it had been, he wouldn't have seemed so afraid, so tender and tentative, like Daniel was a small animal he didn't want to frighten away. Of course,

Daniel could have been wrong. It might have just been the whiskey, making him impulsive.

Daniel couldn't blame what he was feeling on whiskey. This conflict was purely him, his insecurities, as usual. Because that kiss... He'd liked it. Craved more of it in a way he'd never wanted anything physical before. And that meant, had to mean, he was as gay as Asher had said. As all those ex-girlfriends had said. As his parents had suspected. God, he'd been fighting it so long, and here it was, staring him in the face, unavoidable.

He wanted to kiss a man. He wanted more than that. He kept thinking about the way it felt to have Asher's arms around him. The way his heart fluttered when the handsome blond smiled at him or praised him. The incredible color of his eyes. How important his opinion was to Daniel. The way he felt when Asher said his name. The moment Daniel allowed himself to think about it, a torrent of evidence spilled out in front of him. He wanted Asher. Not just because he was a man, but because he was Asher.

Anxiety hit him like a punch to the gut as soon as he confessed it to himself. What did this mean for him? Was he going to have to change now? Become one of those flamboyant people on TV... What if these feelings didn't last beyond getting rescued? What if they got home and Daniel realized he only felt this way because of the situation they were in? What if

Asher decided he'd rather be with someone less troublesome?

Asher didn't exactly seem like the settling down type. The thought made Daniel's heart wrench. He'd been straight all his life. He didn't know how to change now. He didn't know what he was supposed to do. If Asher went away, could he go back to how he was? Or would he find himself running after another man? In the end, would he just be alone, like he always had?

What if he lost his job? He didn't see Donahue being above firing someone for being gay. Would anyone else hire him if they knew? Where would he go? Even if he talked to his family, they would never take him back if they knew. And he'd always wanted kids, a family of his own. Most states still wouldn't let gay people adopt. He couldn't be gay. He couldn't do it. He couldn't risk being alone forever.

Fears and doubts and desires circled around and around in his head as he worked on the clothes, hammering at them until his hands turned numb. When they were clean, he laid them over the rocks to dry and headed back inside, still plagued with insecurity. Asher was sitting near the stove, warming up lunch and looking over a worn map.

"Welcome back," he said, smiling up at Daniel like nothing had happened. "How'd the laundry treat you?"

"I'd sacrifice a few fingers for a laundromat," Daniel answered, sitting next to the other man and warming his hands by the fire. "I may lose them anyway. Figured out where we are yet?"

"I think so," Asher turned the map a little so that Daniel could see. "Based on the stream and the mountains around us, I think we're here, on Mummy Mountain. The stream probably feeds into West Creek, here. Now if we follow West Creek down to the falls, there's a trail there that'll take us down to the Cow Creek Trailhead, where there's bound to be people and phones to call for help."

"But it says here West Creek trail closes in November," Daniel said, worried, as he leaned over the map and pointed out the notation. "What if it's already shut down?"

"It won't be more dangerous than being out here," Asher said. "And the trail head will still be open. We have to try."

Daniel nodded in agreement, though he was still worried, for a variety of reasons.

"We'll leave tomorrow," Asher said, folding up the map, "as long as we feel strong enough and the snow has stopped. We've got enough MREs to last us a while, so there's no need to rush."

"Your stitches are a big concern," Daniel frowned, looking at Asher's side for any sign of blood coming through his sweater. Asher smiled and lifted his shirt to show clean bandages.

"They're holding well," he said, "You did a good job. I'm more worried about your ankle. It's not a good injury to have when you need to hike something like twelve miles."

"I've made it this far," Daniel laughed, trying to ignore the flush of warmth he felt at Asher's concern for him. "I'm not giving up now."

"I didn't think you would," Asher chuckled, mussing Daniel's hair. "But don't worry. I'm feeling so much better I could probably drag you the rest of the way in if I needed to."

"Yeah right. I'll probably end up dragging you in," Daniel shoved Asher playfully. "I've already had you collapse on me once."

"Yeah, so it's your turn!" Asher joked, pushing back, and forgetting about Daniel's dislocated shoulder. When Daniel made a sudden, stunted pain sound, Asher went white, reaching out to steady him. "Shit. Shit, I'm sorry! I forgot!"

Daniel laughed wheezily through his pain.

"It's fine. I'm fine," he promised, waving off Asher's concern. "It's just a bruise."

"I'm sorry, Danny," Asher repeated, and Daniel sensed an apology for more than just the shove behind those words.

"I'm alright," he promised, shaking his head. "And no one in my entire life has ever called me Danny."

"Well, I'm happy to be the first," Asher said primly, leaning closer and pulling at the neck of Daniel's sweater to bare his shoulder.

"What are you doing?" Daniel asked, trying to lean away only to be stopped by Asher sliding an arm around his waist.

"Kissing it better," Asher answered, and touched his lips to Daniel's bruised skin in a delicate kiss. The contact sent a warm shiver through Daniel and he looked away, licking his lips.

"I'm not a child," he muttered. "That's not going to fix anything."

"I don't know," Asher was kissing his way up Daniel's shoulder towards his throat. "It's making me feel better."

Daniel, scarlet, bit his lip to stop an indecent sound from escaping as Asher's lips brushed the hollow of his throat.

"Wow," Asher murmured, awed. "I can feel your pulse. Your heart is beating so fast..." He paused and slowly drew away to meet Daniel's eye. "Are you scared?" he asked. "Do you want me to stop?"

When Daniel nodded, Asher let go at once, withdrawing a bit to give Daniel his space.

"Sorry," Asher spoke softly, like he was talking to a spooked horse. "I shouldn't have sprung that on you. I got carried away."

"It's fine." Daniel was still scarlet with embarrassment, pulling up his sweater and keeping his face turned away.

"Last night, too," Asher continued. "It was wrong of me to force that on you. Disrespectful. It's hard, being this close to you and not being able to... But that's no excuse. I'll keep my distance, I promise."

"It's okay," Daniel insisted. "I'm not upset. I'm just... I'm still not sure about a lot of things."

"Take your time," Asher said, sitting back, and though his voice was understanding, there was hurt in his eyes. "I'm not going anywhere."

Chapter Fourteen

They tip-toed around each other for the second half of the day. But even strained as they were, there was something so pleasantly domestic to Daniel about sharing this space with the other man. Asher's thoughtfulness and consideration were traits that Daniel hadn't expected from the man's initial cowboy attitude. He was quick to back off if he realized something was really bothering Daniel.

They both gave each other the space they both needed. He wasn't as naturally fastidious as Daniel, but he didn't shy away from cleaning up if Daniel asked. Their styles, disparate as they were, seemed to mesh well. And Daniel found he just enjoyed watching the other man, seeing the emotions that crossed his face in everyday moments. Laughter, pensive thought, excitement, frustration. Daniel found all of Asher's reactions fascinating. The man seemed so much more alive than anyone Daniel had ever met.

In the afternoon, Asher rigged up a fishing line with the suture needle and thread and, with a great deal of enthusiasm, went out to try fishing. Daniel decided to stay in and rest his ankle, and instead worked on cataloguing their supplies and what they would be able to take with them. There was a rocking chair, which Daniel had pulled up near the fire, then tugged the kitchen table within reach so that he could sit while sorting out the supplies. He was fairly certain they could turn one of the blankets into a bag. They would take as many of the MREs as they could. The first aid kit of course. The fire starters...

His thoughts drifted back to Asher and he leaned back in his chair. The window was visible when he leaned back far enough, and he could see Asher through it, fussing around by the edge of the stream. It wasn't particularly deep, even at its deepest point, but he might catch something. Even if he didn't, Daniel knew he'd come back red-faced and smiling. That was just the kind of person he was. Daniel wished he could be more like that. More content with his situation regardless of circumstances. Abler to cheerfully push through instead of shutting down. But if he was honest, he knew his admiration for Asher went beyond just wanting to be like him.

He focused on his work, all the familiar anxieties starting up in his head again. It couldn't work. He didn't want to be that person. He was scared of how things would change, scared of taking that label. Scared of a million things, like he was scared of the dark—it was childish and irrational. But he was less scared when Asher was there. And maybe it wouldn't work, but did that make it not worth trying? Things might change when they got home. But this wasn't home, and there was no telling what might happen tomorrow. So why not? Why not?

He clenched his jaw and counted the MRE packets again, his thoughts chasing their tails like frenzied dogs until he couldn't find the energy to care anymore.

"Danny, look!"

Asher burst through the door in a flurry of snow, cheeks red from the cold and a grin on his face, holding a decently sized cutthroat trout. "I actually caught something!" he crowed, pleased with himself.

"I didn't doubt you for a minute," Daniel laughed, feeling his heart lift just looking at the other man. Was it friendship? Attraction? Love? Daniel still couldn't pin down any of his own feelings. "Let's see if we can't figure out a way to cook this thing."

There weren't any dishes or pans left behind, so they improvised something out of MRE wrappers. Asher, with a little difficulty, cleaned the fish, and Daniel, somewhat absurdly, made a breading for it from the MRE crackers. They watched it as it cooked like it was the most entertaining television ever aired, laughing about their luck. Then they shared it, burning their fingers and tongues as they pulled pieces of flaky white flesh away from the bone.

Huddled close to Asher's side, the sweet taste of fresh fish on his lips, Daniel could almost be glad all this had happened. He wanted to be here, right now, exactly like this. He couldn't remember a time when things had felt this right.

"I'm becoming a regular outdoorsman," Asher joked, licking his fingers clean. "When this is over, I might have to retire and become an actual trail guide."

Daniel snorted, sitting back on his hands in satisfaction, feeling full and happy. "After all this, I don't think you could pay me to follow you into the woods," he teased.

"What? I've kept you alive this long," Asher nudged him playfully, avoiding his injured shoulder. "And I'm pretty sure you'd follow me anywhere if I took my shirt off."

"You are way too impressed with your own chest," Daniel rolled his eyes, intending to nudge the other man back but only really succeeding in leaning against him. "It's not that amazing."

"It's pretty amazing," Asher nodded with exaggerated sincerity. "I mean, it managed to draw you in, didn't it? Admit it—you've been wild for it since that day we went swimming."

Daniel groaned, covering his face with his hands, but he was more amused than annoyed. When had Asher's teasing become endearing instead of annoying? When he looked up again Asher was removing his shirt to flex theatrically.

"Stop that," Daniel laughed. "You're going to hurt yourself."

"I'm fine!" Asher protested through his own laughter. "Spoilsport!"

He stopped, but only to put his arm around Daniel and muss his hair. Daniel squirmed to get away and Asher pursued him, laughing against his skin, the tug of fingers at his scalp as his hair tangled around the other man's hand. Daniel froze, realizing how close they were, and stared back into Asher's eyes, separated by only a breath. Asher realized it too, his laughter gradually fading to guilt. He pulled away slowly, his touch brushing Daniel's cheek as his hand left the other man's hair.

"Sorry," his voice was barely above a whisper as he stood, taking the bones of the fish. "I'll go and throw this away."

He turned towards the door and Daniel's heart beat in his throat, demanding he make a decision. All he could think, through the crowding anxieties, was that he didn't want Asher to go. He was standing before he knew it, throwing his arms around Asher's waist. He pressed his forehead to the space between Asher's shoulder blades and closed his eyes, clinging like he thought if he let go the other man would disappear forever.

"I'm not gonna just walk off into the snow," Asher chuckled but couldn't hide the confused distress in his voice. "You don't have to do that just to make me stay."

"I'm not," Daniel, muffled by Asher's shirt, shook his head. "Don't go. Please."

"Danny?" Asher whispered Daniel's name with a kind of reverence "Please don't give me hope where there isn't any. If you aren't sure about this—"

"I'm not scared anymore."

Asher turned in Daniel's arms to look down at him, wary but hopeful.

"I'm not scared," Daniel repeated. "I want this."

Asher had only been waiting for permission. As soon as he had it, he pulled Daniel against him and kissed him hard, his lips warm and demanding, his tongue hot as it explored Daniel's mouth. His hand at the small of Daniel's back slipped lower and Daniel gasped into the kiss as Asher seized him and squeezed, pulling Daniel higher and closer against him.

"C-careful!" Daniel stammered, breaking the kiss as he realized Asher was holding almost all his weight. "You're injured!"

Asher huffed in frustration, his hands still roaming Daniel's skin like he was starved for it, and half carried the other man towards the cot. He sat, pulling Daniel down into his lap, and kissed him again. More prepared now, Daniel returned it, testing the waters. It was an entirely different thing from kissing a woman. He felt like he had to learn how it worked all over again, patiently probing for what worked and what didn't. Asher, desperate as he was, seemed to approve of nearly everything.

140

The hungry graze of his teeth against Daniel's bottom lip left Daniel shivering with approval. His hands slid under Daniel's sweater, a shock of cold at first, quickly forgotten as they roamed Daniel's back, sliding along his spine, tracing the outline of his shoulder blades, playing over his ribs and squeezing at his hips. Daniel shifted, rocking into that touch, and when Asher groaned, he realized how big the bulge he was sitting above had become. He rolled his hips experimentally, feeling the heat of it under him, and Asher's hands stilled, his head on Daniel's shoulder as he trembled under the other man's attention. Daniel felt strangely powerful. He'd never been able to make someone react like that before. He ground down harder and heard Asher curse, the hands on his hips tightening, pushing Daniel down more firmly.

Daniel, flushed with newfound desire, tugged Asher's head up so that he could kiss the other man, hungry and passionate, overwhelmed by how right this felt. He continued to roll his hips against Asher's lap, stroking the other man's trapped bulge with his ass, feeling Asher's desperate moans against his lips. He wanted more. He'd never been so turned on, his own need straining against his pants almost painfully. All his doubts were, for the moment at least, obliterated by sheer lust.

He tugged at the hem of Asher's shirt, dragging it up over his head and throwing it carelessly, finally allowed to touch as he liked, tracing the patterns of Asher's intricate tattoos, his scars, the line of his

141

collarbone. Asher's kisses drifted down to Daniel's throat and Daniel shuddered, suddenly realizing why women liked that so much. He tipped his head back, leaning in as Asher's teeth grazed his jugular. Daniel felt almost dizzy with eagerness.

Asher, who had been fumbling with Daniel's pants, succeeded in getting them open, clumsy in his hurry to shove Daniel's underwear down and pull free his straining shaft. Daniel gasped, whimpering Asher's name as the other man wrapped his hand around him.

"Wait," he said, hand on Asher's chest. The other man stopped at once, waiting for Daniel to push him away. Instead, Daniel began unfastening Asher's pants as well. "You too."

Asher laughed in relief and delight and leaned back to give Daniel better access. Daniel plunged his hand in as soon as he had enough room, a thrill running through him as he felt the heat of another man's tool for the first time. It was embarrassing and a little bit terrifying, but he was too excited to stop.

As he pulled the other man free, his breath caught in surprise, first feeling the weight of it in his hand, then seeing it himself, thick and heavy. Daniel had never considered himself small, on the larger side of average actually. But Asher put him to shame. He looked up from it to stare at Asher, wide eyed.

"If you're getting cold feet we can stop..." Asher offered, though it was clear he would rather say just about anything else. Daniel shook his head.

"No it's fine," he said. "Just more than I expected."

"Don't worry," Asher chuckled, leaning in to kiss him again. "I won't let it hurt you."

"I'm pretty sure it would kill me," Daniel laughed, eyeing the thing like a snake about to bite him.

"Calm down," Asher chuckled. "We're not going that far tonight anyway. I want you able to walk tomorrow after all."

He shifted to lie back on the bed, gently tugging Daniel along to straddle him. One hand caught the cheek of Daniel's behind, the other wrapped around his shaft, squeezing it against Daniel's. Daniel bit his lip at the feeling of the other man's heated flesh against his own, then added both his own hands, forming a tight channel around them. Asher groaned, thrusting up into Daniel's hand, and Daniel felt a rush of pleasure at the slick slide of the other man against him. Asher's hand kneading his backside encouraged him to move his own hips, timing them with Asher's thrusts, moving against each other in hedonistic frenzy.

Asher dragged Daniel's pants lower as they rocked against each other, cursing under his breath as

Daniel whispered his name over and over. Asher's hand slipped back further and Daniel yelped in surprise as he felt a finger pressing against his entrance. He gave Asher an uncertain look but Asher just tugged him closer to kiss him.

"It's okay," he said, gentle and reassuring. "I'm not going to do anything that will hurt you. You're safe with me."

Daniel, despite his nerves, believed Asher completely. He kissed the other man and began moving his hips again, every rock back pushing against Asher's finger, rubbing slow circles on a part of him no one else had ever touched. Aside from being cripplingly embarrassing, it felt good, the sensitive skin lighting up at the contact. He could hardly focus on anything else, the confusion of pleasure and shame occupying his thoughts completely.

He made the mistake of looking down at Asher and saw the other man watching him, blue eyes intense and alive with lust as he stared up at Daniel. Embarrassment crashed down on Daniel like a ton of bricks, realizing how he must look, exposed and needy like this, all of him bared before Asher's eyes.

Suddenly feeling the need to hide, he bent over to press his face into Asher's shoulder. The other man chuckled, but indulged him, running a hand over Daniel's back soothingly. He didn't stop moving his hips, keeping up the steady rhythm of sensation that made Daniel's thoughts cloudy and his voice needy and beyond his control. This close he was practically whimpering into Asher's ear, his hands encircling their heated cocks, squeezing tightly as he felt his limit approaching.

Asher swore and gasped Daniel's name, his thrusts becoming less controlled. He pulled Daniel into a fierce kiss, against which Daniel's needy cries were lost, insignificant when compared to the crash of lips and teeth and tongue that was the two men desperately trying to convey their feelings without words. Daniel shuddered and bucked, pleasure whiting out his vision like the snow storm rising outside. He felt Asher's teeth on his throat and the hot splash of seed on his skin and closed his eyes, thoughts drifting into floating blankness.

Asher shifted to pull Daniel down beside him. He fumbled with numb fingers for a cloth to wipe themselves clean with. Daniel, equally foggy, reached for the blanket, crumpled at the foot of the bed, and pulled it over them as Asher finished his cursory cleanup. Daniel rested with his head on Asher's shoulder, the other man's arm close and comforting around him, and for a moment enjoyed think about absolutely nothing.

Outside, the wind rose to a higher howl. Both men glanced towards the window, where they could see snow whipping past the glass.

"Looks like we might be here a little longer after all," Asher said.

Daniel fell asleep with a smile on his face.

Chapter Fifteen

It snowed straight through the next day. Daniel hardly noticed. He and Asher barely left the bed except to build up the fire and once to clean themselves in vain, knowing they'd dirty themselves again before they'd even finished. Asher couldn't seem to keep his hands to himself the moment he saw Daniel's bare skin, and the myriad little claiming marks he had left on it.

Throughout the day, there was barely a second where they were not touching one another. Daniel curled up between Asher's knees as they ate, lay against his side when they napped, and filled all his thoughts with the other man. If he thought only of Asher, if he stayed completely in this moment, constantly distracted by the sweetness of his kisses and the tempting graze of every touch, then the insecurities gathering in the shadows of his mind couldn't get in.

Outside, the storm raged. But inside, Asher spread Daniel out on the rug in front of the fire and teased him to the edge of madness with lips and tongue and questing fingers. Daniel, back arched and chest heaving with shallow, needy breaths, his skin glistening with sweat in the flickering fire light, tangled his fingers in the golden coils of Asher's hair and dug his heels into the floor. His thoughts were a scrambled, ecstatic mess. Asher slipped a finger inside for the first time and Daniel, surprised, pulled hard enough on Asher's hair that he felt teeth against very sensitive skin. They had to stop for a while, alternately laughing at and scolding each other. But they soon fell together again, and the next time Asher tried it, Daniel was more prepared.

He gave his first blowjob only a little later, sitting on the floor between Asher's knees. His first cock felt heavy on his tongue, while the other man reclined on the cot, petting his hair and coaching him along.

"That's it, use your tongue. Careful, don't go too fast. You don't have to take it all at once. Use your hands and work your way up to it. It's better if you make it last anyway. Shit, yeah, like that. Damn, you look good down there. Anyone ever tell you that you have amazing dick sucking lips? Because..."

He seemed to get a kick out of embarrassing Daniel to death. He'd keep it up until Daniel was scarlet from his ears to his chest and had to give up on whatever he was trying to do to hide his face and groan miserably. At which point Asher would pull Daniel into his lap and kiss whatever part Daniel left exposed, hands or nose or throat, hands teasing and exploring, until Daniel was not just flustered but also aroused beyond reason. The combined sensations would overwhelm him to the point that he lost all self-consciousness and would not just let Asher do whatever he wanted, but beg for it. Asher became an expert in all Daniel's weak points in what felt like record time. After all, they had very little else to focus on but each other.

It wasn't until late that evening, when they finally exhausted themselves completely, that Daniel's thoughts at last had a chance to catch up with him. He laid in Asher's arms, the other man snoring gently beside him, watching the fire burn down to red embers while sleep eluded him. Outside, the wind had finally stopped. Daniel felt curiously numb. The wild joy he'd felt all day—the delicious contentment of not just physical pleasure but affection and the sweet humor of two people fully comfortable with each other—it all drained away and left precisely nothing behind. Daniel had an idea what might replace those feelings, but he was keeping those doors firmly closed for now. So he was numb instead.

On an impulse, he slipped out of Asher's arms and gathered some of the scattered clothing. In his own pants and Asher's sweater, he opened the cabin door and slipped out into the night.

The world was a surreal place after all the snow. Once familiar shapes rendered formless and meaningless under the obfuscation of ice. Daniel couldn't even see the stream. Everything was just whiteness. And then he looked up and saw all that had been erased by the snow was doubled in intensity in the sky.

The night sky wheeled with stars, its color not black but rich dark blues and purples escalating into startling violets, and all of it gleaming with the diamond dust of a thousand million distant silver suns. Daniel, indifferent city dweller, had never seen such a sky. He stumbled a few steps out into the snow, then fell on to his back to just stare up at the splendor in wide-eyed awe. The snow under him soaked through his sweater towards his skin, but he didn't care. It was worth the discomfort to watch this incredible night parade even a moment longer. It was only when he thought that he wished Asher were seeing this too that he remembered those doors he was out here trying to keep closed.

He dragged the neck of the sweater up over the lower half of his face and breathed in Asher's lingering scent, hoping it would help him ignore the feelings that were trying to overcome him. If anything, they made it worse. Because one way or another, this was going to end. They couldn't stay in this cabin, in this moment, forever. Spring would come and force them to change, always. Daniel would remember he wasn't gay, not really, or that he just didn't want to be. Asher would realize he could do far better than a neurotic, insecure nobody...

This was doomed whether Daniel accepted the change in himself or not. And Daniel didn't know which was more frightening. The thought that all of this was just an illusion born out of the desperate situation they were in that, once they were safe, would dissolve like snow in the sunlight? Or the thought of giving into this, of letting himself fall in love with Asher as he knew he was already beginning to, only to find Asher had never invested the weight in it that Daniel had. What was worse—that he might walk away from Asher and feel nothing, or that Asher might walk away from him?

He heard the crunch of snow under feet and his view of the sky was interrupted by the sun, or close enough. Asher smiled down at him from a halo of golden hair, vibrant as Apollo.

"You're going to get sick," Asher pointed out the obvious. "What are you doing out here?"

"I don't know what to do," Daniel confessed. "I feel too many things at once."

"What kind of things?" Asher, seeming to sense this might take a while, sat down in the snow next to him.

"A lot of fear," Daniel confessed, looking up at the sky again. "But I'm happy too. And I regret things. Or will regret them. Or I'm afraid I will regret them. I don't know what I want and everything seems too big to deal with when we're in a situation like this. I don't know if I'll be the same person when I get home."

"You will be," Asher said with absolute certainty, and when Daniel fixed him with a puzzled gaze, he shrugged. "No one ever really changes. People can change their behaviors. But the essential motivations behind them, the person they really are deep down, never changes. An alcoholic starts drinking because they're lonely and when they're drunk they are everyone's friend. But they realize those friendships don't mean anything and they're still lonely, so they join a support group and make friends there, and stop drinking. They changed their behavior, but not the person they are—someone lonely who can't connect with people spontaneously and needs the context of a bar or a group in order to socialize."

"I think you might be oversimplifying things a lot," Daniel said seriously and Asher laughed.

"Yeah, you're right," he agreed. "And I haven't known you that long. But I think I know some of the things that motivate you. I think they're good things. I think you'll still be a good person on the other side of this."

"Could I be someone you'd stay with?" Daniel blurted out before he could stop himself. "After this? Could I be the kind of person you'd want to be with?"

Asher looked surprised, then guilty, glancing away. It was answer enough for Daniel, who wasn't sure if it was a relief or a crushing blow.

"You know the kind of life I live," Asher tried to give Daniel an excuse that would hurt less. "Serious relationships don't really work with what I do. I wouldn't want to drag you into something like that."

"Yeah," Daniel said tonelessly, looking up at the sky.

"Hey."

Asher shifted, leaning over Daniel and planting a big, calloused hand in the snow beside his head.

"What we have right now," Asher stared down at him, brow furrowed with the ferocity of how badly he wanted Daniel to understand and be okay with this. "It isn't nothing. It isn't meaningless just because it can't last forever. You're important. This moment is important. Whatever happens later won't change that."

Daniel didn't answer, too unsure of his own feelings to know what he wanted or why he wanted it. He averted his eyes and remained silent. Asher sighed and sat back on his knees.

"Come on," he said, offering Daniel a hand. "Let's get you back inside before you freeze to death."

Daniel complied, though he still wasn't sure what to feel. He let Asher peel his wet clothes off to hang by the fire, and when the other man began pressing kisses to the still damp skin at the back of his neck, Daniel didn't resist. He threw himself into the act with passion instead, riding Asher's fingers as they thrust against each other. If this was to be all there was, he might as well make the most of it.

Chapter Sixteen

Morning came too soon. The storm that had stopped in the night had not returned and the sun was already beginning to melt the accumulated snow. The awkwardness of the night before melted as well, as Daniel forcibly put it out of his mind. The two men talked and laughed as they ate their breakfast and prepared for a final hike. He would be home soon, Daniel reminded himself. Back to showers and hot food and comfortable beds. He was looking forward to all of those things more than he could say. So why did he feel so reluctant to leave behind this dusty abandoned cabin?

He looked back with growing reluctance as Asher shut the door behind them, and the other man smiled, mussing Daniel's hair.

"Chin up, Danny," he said. "Let's get home, and when we're both in better shape, I'll take you camping out here again."

Daniel huffed with tired humor. "We could make it an annual thing," he suggested as they started walking, following the stream. "Once a year we jump in a river and get lost in the woods together."

"Sounds like a great time to me," Asher agreed. "I've always wanted to have sex on the very top of a mountain."

Daniel sputtered and Asher laughed, and together they started on their way down the mountain.

Asher had found a sturdy pine branch the day before and stripped it for Daniel to use as a walking stick. It helped a great deal with keeping the weight off of his ankle. They made decent progress, following the narrow stream down the forested slopes.

Daniel was happy to see the snow disappearing quickly as they descended, until soon it lingered only in shadowed patches. When the trees opened up into swaths of rocky grassland there was no snow at all. The stream quickly shed its skin of ice and rolled along in noisy excitement.

Once, as they were passing through a copse of cottonwood trees, a herd of elk burst through the brush ahead of them, crashing in a wild stampede through the trees and bounding away across the hill. Asher and Daniel threw themselves out of the way of the flying hooves, landing hard in the dirt with Asher's arm around Daniel protectively. They watched the elk leap with alien grace over bracken and briar, close enough to feel the heat radiating from their huge brown bodies. Their eyes, huge and dark, stared forward almost sightlessly, gazing into the future forest towards some animal need Daniel couldn't understand. Asher held him until the last of their eerie bugling cries had echoed into nothingness. Then they stood and carried on, in speechless awe of what they'd seen.

Daniel felt like his eyes were more open now, since the cabin. Before the river, he'd been too focused on his own misery to see anything but the most basic frame of nature's beauty, and only in the context of wishing for a situation where he could enjoy it more. Now he was witness to all the minutiae of forest life. The scamper of animals. The curious constructs of intertwining plant life. The play and pattern of light, soft as it touched on things it had graced the same for millions of years, compared to the confused way it fumbled on the explosion of human civilization, so recent and so strange. So ceaselessly self-referential and inward turned, unable to see even nature as anything but a reflection of their own virtues and fears. What a weird existence, Daniel thought. What a bizarre thing to be. As he thought this, he smiled at Asher, for once perfectly happy to be so far from normalcy.

Disaster, though expected, never arrived. The stream met the creek as Asher had hoped it would, and they turned to follow it east, both of them feeling optimistic for the first time since the river. The water, a deep jade green beside them, rolled on through increasingly cultivated land, open grassy places where Daniel was certain farms must have once existed, interrupted by bouts of dense, tangled forest. The fact that they would be out soon began to feel more real. Somehow it had seemed too strange without the drama of a rescue. But here they were, almost home. They hurried on, excitement pushing them to go faster than they really should have.

Asher, in his eagerness, put on his trail guide mask again, pointing out different bird and plant species they passed. He'd learned a lot in a few hours googling while in the airport on the way here.

"Look, that's a kestrel circling! And that's a three toed wood pecker! Did you know the American three toed woodpecker breeds farther north than any other American woodpecker? The only bird in the world that breeds higher up than them is the Eurasian three toed woodpecker, which used to be considered the same species. They're functionally identical except for mitochondrial differences, which is why they were split. I remembered that because I think it's dumb as shit."

Now that his trivia was no longer sprinkled with teasing insults, Daniel actually found it rather entertaining. His enthusiasm was contagious, and once in a while Daniel would chip in with something he remembered from the brochures.

"There's a mountain chickadee," Asher pointed out, gesturing towards a tiny gray and black bird, sunning itself on a branch with its feathers fluffed out to absorb as much warmth as possible. "They live in the park year round."

"I read they only need to eat about ten calories a day," Daniel added, pausing to watch the little bird. "Too bad we can't do that."

"Would have made this nightmare of a trip a lot easier," Asher laughed, then put an arm around Daniel with a wink. "And a lot more fun. Did you know a teaspoon of cum can be up to seven calories?"

"Oh my god." Daniel squirmed away, red in the face and laughing.

"Think about it!" Asher shouted, hurrying after him. "You could live on two blow jobs a day!"

Around noon, they stopped by the edge of the creek to eat. The MREs had, by now, rather lost their novelty, but Daniel's brush with starvation had been recent enough that he could continue to choke down MREs for a good while before he got sick of them. That didn't stop him from flicking cold, flaccid bits of spaghetti at Asher across their impromptu picnic spread. He cheered as one splattered perfectly against the side of the other man's cheek.

"Keep that up and I'm gonna pour this absurdly small bottle of tabasco down your throat," Asher threatened, grinning.

The next piece of spaghetti landed precisely on the bridge of his nose. "That's it!"

He tackled Daniel before the other man could do more than shriek, twisting off the cap of the hot sauce as Daniel laughed and struggled to get away, pushing at his chest and squirming. Asher pushed his fingers past Daniel's lips, forcing the smaller man's mouth open. Daniel felt an unexpected thrill at the sensation of Asher's finger pushing down his tongue, the weight of the other man pinning him down making his heart race. His temporary excitement was quickly forgotten as hot sauce poured down his throat. He howled in exaggerated pain and indignation at the burn while Asher laughed victoriously.

"If I'm going down," Daniel gasped, "you're going down with me!"

He grabbed Asher by the head and pulled him into a deep kiss, making certain to spread as much of the hot sauce as he could until Asher successfully pulled away, gasping and whining. Mouths and lungs burning, the two men rolled in the grass beside each other, tears stinging their eyes and wheezy laughter echoing through the valley until they could speak again.

"My tongue still feels numb," Asher complained later as they pushed through the thorny chaparral, Daniel using his stick to flatten the meanest looking snares so they could pass. "I might never taste again. What will you do if you've killed my sense of taste forever?"

"You already didn't have any taste," Daniel teased, smiling at the other man.

"Well that explains why I can't get enough of you," Asher teased back, and Daniel rolled his eyes. "I'm serious. I still can't feel anything—"

With a sigh, Daniel turned and kissed the other man hard, his tongue sliding wetly against Asher's. When he pulled away, Asher was staring down at him with undisguised desire, licking his lips.

"Oh. There it is."

Daniel chuckled and turned away to keep walking. Asher followed him, a glint in his eye that promised he would pin Daniel against a tree soon. A few steps later however, the tangle of briar and young trees gave way to an open meadow, rolling even in this late season with a riot of color, the red gold leaves of birch all the fierer against sweeps of aster and forget me not. A young elk, nosing the clover on the far end of the little clearing, startled and fled as Daniel and Asher stumbled out of the bracken. A hare, less wary, mottled brown and white as it grew its winter coat, froze and watched them.

Daniel stumbled out into the clearing, eyes wide, and looked back at Asher with a grin. He didn't need to say anything. He could see the wonder in Asher's eyes. The other man took two long strides towards him and pulled him close, kissing him tenderly in the warmth of the early afternoon sun that dappled the ethereal meadow.

They tumbled together into the sweet smelling grass, hands worshipping one another without any real goal, neither of them in any rush. There was a sense of mortality, a feeling that this might be their last opportunity, and a mutual desire to make it last if they could. They took their time, crushing the flowers beneath them and rolling in the fertile scent, their hands wandering over landscapes now well-known but not yet familiar and still full of secrets to discover. Asher's fingers slid over Daniel's ribs like the keys of a piano, playing him delicately. Daniel learned and relearned the shape of Asher's jaw and the sweet hollow of his throat with lips alone. Asher pulled Daniel over him to relish the reassuring weight of the smaller man's body pressed along the length of his own, and Daniel reversed them, tugging the tie out of Asher's hair so that it would tumble around him and he could hide within its curtains of gold.

When eventually clothes began to fall to the wayside, they were removed almost with reluctance, like unwrapping the last present on Christmas Day, knowing it signaled the approach of the end. Asher would remove nothing without covering every inch of skin he bared in kisses. Daniel drank in the sight of the other man like he was water in the desert, like oxygen, trying to memorize everything he saw, from the way the sun gleamed on Asher's skin, to the white aster clinging to his hair and scattered across the intricate darkness of his tattoos.

They bared each other completely and lay revealed to the glory of nature and each other, sun bathing their skin. Daniel was struck with a sudden shyness to be so exposed in the open light of day, but Asher refused to let him hide his face, tugging his hands away to shower him in kisses. Laying in a bed of forget me not and fragrant thyme, Daniel held his breath and counted every silvered kiss Asher pressed to his skin as the other man trailed his way down Daniel's trembling body towards the heat at his center. He dragged a burning tongue up the underside of Daniel's shaft and Daniel's hips rose to follow and prolong the delicious contact. Asher kissed the blushing head of Daniel's cock before he engulfed it. Daniel, shivering and overwhelmed by the sudden enveloping heat, sighed his name and clung to Asher's hair like gravity had vanished and it were all that was holding him to the earth. Asher's mouth rose and fell over him in measured passes, deep and slow, a gradual escalation of pleasure that promised it would not be over for a very long time. Daniel shuddered and arched, bucking for more, but Asher's hand on his hip pinned him in place like a trapped butterfly while the other man took his time in devouring him.

Just as Daniel felt himself tipping over the edge of the world into glittering oblivion, Asher pulled away. Daniel, breathless and whining, looked up to protest, to see Asher bending to fetch something from their bag, sun highlighting the bow of his ribs as he stretched. He returned with a packet of petroleum jelly from the first aid kit.

"I made sure to bring this with us," he chuckled, opening it. "Just in case."

He squeezed a portion of the jelly on his fingers and, before Daniel had time to question what he was up to, he'd leaned down to swallow Daniel again while his fingers pressed into Daniel's entrance below. Eased by the slick lubricant, Daniel was surprised how much more quickly he adjusted to the sting of intrusion. There had been a certain illicit thrill to this even before but, now that he wasn't distracted by the discomfort, it was all the more pleasant, even pleasurable. It was a strange stimulation, embarrassing in how vulnerable it made him feel, the sensitivity different from anything he was used to. And then Asher curled his fingers just the right way and Daniel, caught off guard by the bolt of pleasure that shot through him, shouted in surprise, hips jerking upward into Asher's mouth as he nearly came.

Asher pulled away from him to chuckle and wipe his mouth with the back of his hand. Daniel stared at him, flustered and only just beginning to put together what that must have been. Asher smiled at him and pressed that place again, admiring the way Daniel gasped and squirmed at the nearly electric waves of stimulation that rushed through him. His mouth found Daniel's cock again, but he went slower now, just keeping Daniel in edge while he added a third and then a fourth finger, stretching Daniel open, teasing that place inside him even as his tongue played against the underside of Daniel's head relentlessly. Daniel was soon barely aware of any discomfort, thinking of nothing but how desperately he needed to cum. Asher seemed to decide the time was about right as well. He'd been holding back, teasing, and now he dove in, engulfing Daniel until the other man's cock nudged the back of his throat.

Daniel choked on the sounds of desperate pleasure that welled up in him at the dual stimulation, shuddering and crying Asher's name as the other man pushed him so suddenly over the edge of orgasm that he felt like he was falling, tumbling head over heels into ecstasy, the same way he'd fallen into this relationship. Daniel tried to gasp a warning to the other man, but Asher only swallowed Daniel more deeply, milking him of every last drop.

Asher pulled away slowly as Daniel caught his breath, aftershocks and tremors of ecstasy still running through him like he was lying on a live wire.

"You didn't," he shivered, "have to do that."

"I need the calories." Asher winked playfully and shifted to kneel over Asher, kissing him softly. Daniel blushed as he tasted himself, but his attention was quickly diverted by Asher's hand under his knees, lifting his legs.

"Do you think you can?" Asher asked, and Daniel shivered as he felt the press of a hot brand against his entrance. "It's alright if you're not ready."

"No, I can do it," Daniel said quickly, before his nerves could get the better of him. He spread his legs wider for the other man, scarlet to his ears. "I can do it."

Asher swallowed hard and Daniel could practically see the desperate excitement in his eyes as he spread the rest of the lubricant on himself. "Let me know if you need to stop," Asher fixed Daniel with a serious look. "The minute anything doesn't feel right, okay? I don't want to hurt you."

Daniel nodded, but he couldn't quite form words at the moment, his thoughts focused on Asher's thick tool, currently glistening with lubricant and aiming for a place very unused to such intrusions. He thought his heart might explode. As he felt the first stretch of Asher pushing forward, he closed his eyes tight and gripped the grass, holding his breath. Asher stopped at once, leaning down to kiss Daniel's scrunched, anxious lips.

"Relax," he murmured, soothing. "I can't do anything while you're that tense. You'll be okay, Danny. I promise."

Slowly, as Asher stroked Daniel's chest and whispered reassurances, Daniel calmed down. As the tension eased, Asher slid forward, slow and careful. It burned, but not intolerably so. And Daniel knew now what could exist beyond the discomfort if he held out. He took deep breaths, the scent of grass and of the man over him filling his senses. The feeling of being spread open and filled this way was overwhelming beyond anything he could define, drowning out even the sting of the stretch. There was something shamefully satisfying in it, the weight and fullness, that Daniel worried he might become hooked on.

Asher took his time, pausing often and letting Daniel adjust. His hips worked in little circles whenever he stopped moving forward, getting Daniel used to the motion, and occasionally his little stirring motions would press against that place inside Daniel again, making him tighten and squirm, sparks of pleasure like little fireworks erupting across his skin. By the time he was fully sheathed, Daniel was hard again, flushed and biting his lip, gripping the grass in order to fight the urge to touch himself. Asher was inside him, thick and heavy and impossible to ignore, making Daniel dizzy with a desire he'd never felt before but wanted so much it was enough to make him almost crazy.

Asher stopped, holding still inside Daniel though both of them were desperate to move, giving the other man time to get used to the sensation, and to the burn that accompanied it. "How are you feeling?" he asked, breathless, stroking Daniel's stomach with a shaking hand. "Do you think you can handle it if I move?"

"Please," Daniel insisted with a frantic nod. "Please, do it."

Asher shifted at once, pulling back in a slow slide that left Daniel shivering and feeling strangely empty. And then the other man slid forward again, a smooth, quick strike that Daniel felt all the way up his spine, making his heart skip in his chest. He gasped, babbled Asher's name, and the other man pulled back to thrust again. Daniel, completely overwhelmed, clung to Asher's shoulders and shook with every blow. Even the ones that missed the place inside of him that sent fireworks rushing under his skin had their own kind of pleasure. There was the strange stimulation of having his insides stirred up this way. His cock bounced and dripped with every driving thrust in, the rushes of wild, unexpected pleasure dizzying.

Asher was whispering a litany of curses, his expression an agony of pleasure as he tried to hold back, to draw this out further. He leaned over and Daniel caught the other man's mouth in a sloppy, distracted kiss, groaning as the angle of Asher's thrusts changed. Asher caught both of Daniel's hands, lacing their fingers as he rocked his hips against the deepest parts of Daniel's core. Daniel made an attempt to roll his hips as well and match the other man's pace, but it was difficult to do anything but lay there and feel it, every thrust scattering his thoughts to the winds.

Asher let go of one of Daniel's hands in order to catch the smaller man's hips instead, tilting them up for a different angle, one that drove against Daniel's spot even more solidly than before. Daniel cursed, throwing his head back as hot, liquid pleasure rushed through him, repeating Asher's name like he was begging. Asher throbbed inside him and Daniel knew the other man was close. Unable to resist any longer, Daniel reached up to stroke himself, twitching and tightening around Asher as he felt himself approaching his own end. Asher stared down at him, taking in the wanton image of Daniel flushed and spread open and desperately seeking his own climax. Daniel, too wrapped up to be embarrassed, stared back, crying Asher's name as he came, splashing his own seed across his chest and tightening around the man inside him. Asher, a few wild thrusts later, buried himself as deeply in Daniel as he could. Daniel watched Asher's face in rapturous awe as the other man came, pouring himself out inside Daniel in a hot flood. Daniel could feel it within him and the realization was almost shocking.

Asher pulled Daniel close as he finished, burying his face in the smaller man's dark hair and breathing deeply while he came down. Daniel clung to him tightly, lightheaded and feeling strangely empty without Asher inside him. Not to mention sore. He'd probably feel that a lot later. But for now he'd never felt so content.

"I could do that forever," Asher chuckled, nuzzling Daniel's ear.

"I'm in," Daniel replied, and though he'd meant it to be part of the joke, it came out more serious than he meant to. Asher pulled back a little to look Daniel in the eye, gauging how honest he was being.

"Danny..." he said slowly, but Daniel cut him off, rolling away.

"I know! I know..." Daniel sat up and reached for his clothing. "You're not the kind of guy who does commitment. I'm not the kind of guy you change for..."

Asher put his arms around Daniel from behind, kissing the back of his neck. "I'm sorry," he said, and Daniel could hear the aching sincerity in his voice.

"Me too," Daniel agreed. "I spoiled the mood again." He turned back with a sad smile and kissed Asher, tender and lingering, then pulled away and began to dress himself.

"I'll probably forget about this when I'm home anyway. I'll just go back to how I was..."

Asher leaned past him to tug Daniel's shirt out of his hands. When Daniel turned, Asher kissed him, and pushed him down into the grass again.

The second time was rougher, more desperate, and silent.

Chapter Seventeen

They stayed in the meadow for the night, making their shelter against a large tree. Now that they were so much further down the mountain, there was almost no risk of snow, so they slept without worry, curled up together in the same sleeping bag. Dawn over the meadow the next morning was beautiful, mist winding through the birch and aster.

Daniel was an expert at ignoring his feelings. They carried on following the creek as though there was no conflict between them at all. They were only slightly quieter than they had been yesterday.

"Your limping is worse," Asher observed, frowning. "Is your ankle bothering you?"

"Not quite," Daniel laughed. "It's something else that's sore."

"Oh, right." Asher turned a little red, though he was grinning. "Sorry about that. Want me to carry you?"

"I'll be fine." Daniel rolled his eyes.

"I really don't mind." Asher tried, opening his arms like he expected Daniel to just leap into them.

"Asher!" Daniel, exasperated, sighed. "I got this far with enough bruises and fractures to choke a horse. I think I'll survive a little post coital soreness!"

Asher gave up, embarrassed.

"Besides, it's not that much further anyway, is it?" Daniel pulled the map from his pocket and unfolded it, checking where he thought they were against the landmarks. "We'll be at the falls soon. And that's less than four miles from the trail head. Look, you can see the water speeding up before the falls."

The stream, which had been mostly placid until now, had grown more quick and shallow as it approached its end. Daniel felt a rush of excitement tempered by regret. He ignored both.

"I think they might be just past this wood here," Asher mused, peering at the map as the trees began to thicken around them again. "If that's the right mountain then—"

A distant yell—the unmistakable sound of a human voice—echoed in the distance. Asher and Daniel looked at each other once, then took off towards it, rushing in their delight.

"Carter!" They heard more clearly as they got closer. "Price!"

"It's a search team!" Daniel said, elated. "They're looking for us!"

They rushed towards the voices, hearts pounding, Daniel limped ahead of Asher so that the larger man wouldn't leave him behind.

"Hey!" Daniel tried to call out, breathless and stumbling from the effort. "Hey!"

But his calls seemed to blend in with the search party's or get caught on the wind. He gave up, saving his breath for his limping run, leaning heavily on his walking stick, his ankle protesting every step as it had been for days.

"Daniel," Asher, hurrying after him, called out, quiet but insistent. "Daniel. Danny!"

He grabbed Daniel by the shoulder, dragging him to a stop. Daniel turned, confused, and started to ask why, but Asher put a finger to his lips. "Something doesn't feel right," Asher said, "Just humor me for a second, okay?"

Daniel frowned, but if he couldn't trust Asher after all this, then what was the point of any of it? He nodded, staying quiet as Asher took the lead, moving cautiously forward through the underbrush. Soon they heard voices again, not far ahead of them.

"Carter! Price! Are you out here?"

Daniel's eyes widened as he realized it was Donahue's voice. He'd never expected his boss to be out here personally searching for him. He started to step forward, but Asher put out a hand to stop him, giving him a look to keep him silent.

"Sir, it's been days."

Daniel, after a moment, recognized secretary Susan's voice.

"I'm certain if they were alive they would have been found by now."

"I can't just give up, Susan!" Donahue scolded the woman. Daniel saw the couple come into view a little distance away, moving between the trees with flashlights though it was early in the day. Asher pulled Daniel down beneath the cover of the bracken. "If the bodies haven't turned up then there's still a chance they're alive!"

Daniel smiled, touched by Donahue's unexpected concern. Asher's concern had obviously been misplaced.

"And if they're still alive, I have to kill them myself!"

Daniel's blood went cold.

"By which you mean, have me kill them, sir."

"Of course Susan, don't be absurd. I'm a gentleman! I don't do my own murdering."

"Of course not, sir. In that case, would it not be more efficient to just wait and let the wilderness take care of them?"

"And risk one of them wandering out alive and word getting back to the Family that I threw their enforcer into the rapids in a leaky raft? Or worse! Someone might actually find the bodies! If I'm going to convince the Family that their man ran off with the money I owed them, Asher Price has to disappear completely! And that means I have to find the bodies first. And if they aren't bodies yet, they will be."

Asher gave Daniel a significant look and Daniel, a little weak kneed, leaned on him to keep himself upright. Mr. Donahue was trying to kill him?

"Besides," Donahue sniffed self-importantly, his voice getting more faint as he moved away from Daniel and Asher's hiding place, "diligently searching makes me look good."

"It would make you look better sir if you were doing it with the rest of the search teams on the Roaring River."

"Well, their bodies aren't going to show up on a river I didn't put them in, are they Susan? Really, use that big brain I hired you for."

The two continued to bicker, occasionally calling out for the missing men, until their voices receded into the distance. When it was safe, Daniel slumped to the ground.

"Holy shit."

"Holy shit is a vast understatement."

Asher sank to the ground next to Daniel, running a hand through his hair, eyes wide.

"I can't believe Mr. Donahue wants to kill me." Daniel let his head rest against the tree behind him, stunned beyond any other reaction.

"Me either," Asher agreed, "I never would have thought that little weasel had the balls. We're going to have to change up our plans."

"What, why?" Daniel sat forward, frowning at Asher. "We're almost out! We can take Mr. Donahue, right?"

"Probably," Asher shrugged, "but not Susan. I've seen that woman's arrest record. She's terrifying. She has killed before and she will again. I'm not going anywhere near her without serious firepower."

Daniel was taken aback for a moment, trying to imagine Donahue's tidy, efficient secretary as 'terrifying.' She did always have a way of appearing where you least expected her.

"So what do we do?" Daniel asked as Asher stood, accepting the other man's hand when he offered it. "Do we keep looking for the trail?"

"He'll have someone watching it," Asher ran a hand over his face in frustration. "If we just blunder out we'll walk right into his hands. We have to get to a phone, but even if we get out of this park, he'll just keep trying. That Susan is relentless."

"Can't we call the cops?" Daniel asked, searching for a way out of this mess. "If we tell them Donahue is planning to kill us, they'll protect us, right?"

"We don't have any evidence," Asher shook his head. "It'd be our word against his. And his word is backed up by a lot of money and high priced lawyers. We won't win. Plus, if the Family finds out I didn't get his money and let him get away without so much as throwing a punch, they'll be after us too."

He leaned against the trunk of a tree, and Daniel saw him fumbling for a cigarette he didn't have. Daniel leaned against a tree across from him, the gap between them wide and stark. Daniel contemplated that distance while Asher, muttering and wishing for nicotine, focused on a plan that could save them.

All Daniel could think about was the things they were refusing to say, the fears they were refusing to deal with. They got along so well so long as they didn't talk about it. If he ignored the disappointment on the horizon, he could be happy with Asher. Happier than he'd been for most of his life. But that couldn't last. As soon as they left these woods, reality would be there to spoil everything. He stared across the gap at Asher, heart aching as he tried to come to terms with the inevitable ending to all of this. Eventually, Asher stopped grumbling about how this was not the way he'd planned to quit smoking, and noticed Daniel's stare.

"What's wrong?" he asked, concern drawing lines between his brows.

"What if we just left?" Daniel tried, heart pounding with futile hope. "Forget Donahue and the mob and everything else. The world thinks we're dead. We could go anywhere. Just start over, you and me."

He expected the look of guilt and pity on Asher's face, but that didn't make it hurt any less.

"You know that wouldn't work, Danny," Asher said, like he was breaking the news that Santa wasn't real to a child who should have figured it out by now. "Even if the Family wouldn't come after my head, we wouldn't get far with no money or identities. It's not that easy to just abandon your life and start again."

"We could try," Daniel pushed, the corners of his mouth pulled down in grim desperation. "I've got some savings. We'll go somewhere they don't care about who we are. An island somewhere. Or a mountain. If we could live out here, we could make it work."

Asher sighed, looking away and rubbing at his eyes. "No, we can't," he insisted. "You think camping out for a few days means you're prepared to be homeless and hunted by the mob? I won't put you in danger like that."

Daniel's hands tightened on the hem of his sweater, clutching it in white-knuckled fists. "Are you saying that because it wouldn't work," his blood was rushing in his ears and his voice came out louder than he meant it to, "or because you don't want to be with me?"

Asher looked stunned for a moment, caught off guard by Daniel's intensity. "Danny, you know it isn't... Look, we can deal with this later."

"No! I'm tired of pretending this isn't a problem." Daniel was shaking with something between heartbreak and indignant anger. "I can't just pretend this is enough for me. It's not like I blame you for me not being good enough. I'm not an idiot. I know I'm nothing special."

"Danny, that's not true—"

"Stop trying to save my feelings," Daniel demanded, pinning Asher with a fiery, wounded glare. "I'm not a kid or some fragile thing you have to take care of. You keep putting it off like it'll be easier for me if you ditch me as soon as we get home. I know what I am, Asher. I'm bitter and lonely and weird and up until a few days ago I thought I was straight. Now I try to think about going back to how my life was before, to living any kind of life without you in it, and it feels like dying."

He paused to push back the angry tears that tried to overcome him at the thought of the empty, lonely life he'd lived before this. Asher, his expression tortured with guilt, reached out, then thought better of it, opened his mouth to say something, but couldn't find the words.

"I don't expect you to spend the rest of your life with someone like me," Daniel's voice was choked, but he pushed the words out anyway. "I just can't stand to keep pretending everything is fine. It hurts, thinking about what it could be like, when I know it won't happen. So if you won't stay with me when this is over, if you don't want to be with me, just tell me now and stop pretending. That's all I'm asking. Just get it over with now."

Asher just stared at him for a long moment, conflicting emotions rioting across his handsome features. Hurt and guilt and shame boiled up towards anger while Daniel watched.

"You're so full of shit," Asher blurted out at last, startling Daniel. "You're honestly going to stand there and say *you're* not good enough for *me*? Were you not listening when I told you I work for the mob? Do you think I can just settle down with someone while I'm living that kind of a life? That we could have some kind of cute domestic fantasy while I'm breaking kneecaps on the weekends? It was never going to be anything but a fling because I can't be with anyone. I can't put anyone through that. Especially not someone I… Someone I genuinely like!"

Daniel listened in silence, his expression frozen in a look of angry hurt.

"Try to understand…" Asher pushed his hair back with a frustrated sigh. "The more I liked you, the more I've realized I can't risk being with you. The worse it would be if you got hurt because of me."

Daniel just shook his head. "Fine," he hissed. "Fine! If it's so painful to be around each other, then I'll leave! I'll go and find Donahue. It's you he wants dead after all. He doesn't care about me. So just figure out your own way home. It'll probably be easier without me."

"Danny, don't—" Asher tried to protest as Daniel hobbled onto his walking stick and started to limp away. Asher reached for Daniel's shoulder and Daniel knocked his hand away.

"Don't touch me!" Daniel snapped. "I don't ever want to feel that again. Just leave me alone!"

Chapter Eighteen

It took almost an hour for Daniel, limping, to find Donahue and Susan.

"Carter!" Donahue called in surprise as Daniel stumbled out of the underbrush. "We've been worried sick! Is Price with you?"

Daniel shook his head, exhausted, as Donahue hurried closer, gesturing for Susan to help Daniel stand.

"Did he survive the river?" Donahue asked. "It's been days! We were getting ready to give up on you."

"Does it matter?" Daniel leaned on Susan, his eyes evasive. "He's not here. Are there medical people with you? I could really use some pain killers."

"Of course it matters!" Donahue scoffed. "We can't rescue only one of you! Even if you've only seen his body, just to know what happened would be a comfort, I'm sure."

"Asher's alive," Daniel said, tired and bitter as he leaned on Susan's shoulder. "He's not far away. We had an argument and split up just a little while ago. Where's the rest of the search party?"

"You two really don't get along, do you?" Donahue muttered. "To split up in a situation like this."

"We couldn't agree on which way to go," Daniel said, shrugging. "Is your car near? I've sprained my ankle and I'd kill for some real food..."

"We should find Asher first, don't you think?" Donahue steered Daniel back the way he had come. "We can't leave him wandering out here if he's nearby."

"Sir," Susan, supporting Daniel on one side, interrupted, "wouldn't it make more sense to have him wait with the truck? He's injured. He'll slow us down."

"Don't be silly, Susan!" Donahue said too loudly. "Carter here is tough as nails! He'd never leave a job half done. How many times did you go through that financial paperwork I told you to just sign and send to records?"

"Three times, sir," Daniel replied absentmindedly, looking tired and worried. "But really, if we could just go home..."

"Hang in there, Carter!" Donahue clapped him on the shoulder too hard to be encouraging. "I'm sure Price won't be far. Then we can all get out of here. We can go for burgers."

"I would really rather go to the hospital."

"Nonsense! All you need is some rest and a good American burger! Now, which direction is he in?"

Daniel, unable to fight Donahue's insistence, allowed himself to be propelled back into the woods,

183

tiredly pointing them back in the direction he'd come from. Asher wouldn't be there anymore anyway, and at this point, it hardly mattered. Daniel wanted so badly to just lie down and sleep for a week.

"So, how did you and Asher make it this far?" Donahue asked, a hand on Daniel's back keeping him moving forward even when he wanted to stop. "That river must have done a real number on you. I can see the bruises from here."

"It did," Daniel sighed tiredly. "It kicked our shit in to be honest."

"Language, Carter!" Donahue laughed. "Price must have rubbed off on you."

"We wanted to stay by the river and wait for rescue," Daniel went on, "but a bear chased us off and we lost track of the river completely. We had to hike a couple of days to even figure out where we were again. Then we got caught in a blizzard and had to hole up in an abandoned ranger station for a few days. But we found a map that helped us figure out how to get back."

"Well aren't you two just a pair of lucky ducks!" Donahue said, smiling with no humor in his eyes. "Anyone else would have died three times over. You know, you should write an autobiographical book about your experience. People love those. You'll make a mint."

Daniel hung his head a little, thoughts far away, back in that cabin. That wasn't something he really wanted to think about right now, much less share with other people. "Right now," he said, trudging along under Susan's calculating gaze, "I don't really care about anything but getting home. I just want to sleep."

"You'll get your nap soon Carter," Donahue promised ominously. "The sooner we find Price, the sooner you can rest."

"He's not going to be where I left him anyway," Daniel complained. "He'll have moved on, looking for his own way back to the trail."

"Does he have the map?" Donahue asked, frowning.

"No," Daniel admitted with a frustrated sigh, "We fought over it when we split up and it got torn to pieces. I have parts of it, but not enough to make it useful."

"Well that will make things a little more difficult," Donahue said, but he sounded relieved. Daniel was sure he was glad Asher was less likely to stumble out of the woods and into other people before Donahue found him.

Before long, they reached the copse where Daniel and Asher had split. Tattered pieces of map still littered the ground, blown against the net of briar by the wind. Daniel watched them flutter, mouth pulled down by the unpleasant reminder.

"Where did he go from here?" Donahue asked impatiently. "Which direction did he go in?"

"Give me a minute," Daniel sighed, sitting down against a tree. "I've been hiking on a sprained ankle for days. Give me a minute to rest."

Donahue huffed impatiently, muttering about wasted time, but Daniel didn't budge, closing his eyes. He could almost still hear the angry words he and Asher had exchanged echoing in the branches, and they stabbed at him like a knife. He hadn't been wrong. But guilt still ate at him, insisting that two minutes together in willfully ignorant bliss was better than being apart. Daniel's worries nagged at him, wondering where Asher was and if he was going to be okay. Daniel was sure Asher would move much faster without Daniel to slow him down. But the worry stayed anyway. Hopefully it would fade with time. Donahue would give up hunting after a while, and he would get a proper doctor to look at his injuries, and then he would go home and sleep, possibly forever.

"Alright, alright, that's enough resting," Donahue pulled Daniel to his feet impatiently and hurried them on. "We've got to keep going. Don't you know a man's life could hang in the balance?"

"Alright, alright, we're going," Daniel muttered. "He'll be fine though. He's a trail guide, you know. He could survive out here for weeks probably."

"Yeah, I wouldn't be so sure about that," Donahue laughed dryly. "We should find him."

They kept going as the morning wore on towards mid-day. Daniel had to stop often, his ankle beginning to reach a point where it just wouldn't support him anymore.

"When we argued," Daniel said during one of his breaks, "Price said there was a trail on the map closer than the one at West Creek Falls. He wanted to head this direction and find it. I wasn't so sure."

"Well, I'm not seeing any sign of a trail this way," Susan pointed out.

"He's stubborn," Daniel said with the weariness of experience "He'll keep going this way till he finds it or something else stops him."

That stubbornness would probably get him killed, Daniel thought, his stomach twisting at the idea. He didn't want to see that.

"Then we'll keep going this way," Donahue agreed through gritted teeth. "We're bound to catch up to one lost, injured man eventually."

"Not when we're dragging an injured man of our own," Susan pointed out, eyeing the GPS in her hand over her cat eye glasses. "He's slowing us down too much, sir." She gave Donahue a significant look, but he shook his head.

"Fine," the man said, throwing his hands up. "Carter. Sit there. Susan and I are going to go ahead. We'll circle back if we don't see any sign of him in, what would you say Susan, an hour or so?"

Susan nodded and the two of them turned to leave.

"Wait," Daniel called. "Leave me the radio. If you two get lost, I'll need a way to call for help."

Donahue huffed impatiently and threw the walkie into Daniel's lap.

"Just don't lose it!" he hissed, then hurried away, Susan looking back at Daniel suspiciously before pacing after her boss.

Daniel sighed once they were gone. He settled back against a tree, glad for the opportunity to really relax, the radio held lightly in his hand. He wondered, worried, if they might find Asher. If they did, would they come back for Daniel at all? Or just leave him out here, a useless inconvenience...

Chapter Nineteen

Several hours later and a several miles away, golden late afternoon was turning bruise colored as evening settled over the Cow Creek Trail Head. It was a stoic image in autumn, brown and stark, the old ranch that marked it a solemn and solitary place of dusty historical plaques and little life. A dirt parking lot was empty except for a single, extravagant truck. Donahue's other two secretaries sat in its spacious cab, trading smokes and griping about being made to do this at all. They were both certain they didn't have much longer to wait. It was getting dark and Donahue would not continue looking in the dark. He'd ask them to come and pick him up soon, driving the fat, overbuilt truck over the hiking trail heedless of the signs posted that warned them against just that.

In the meantime, they were keeping watch, waiting to see if any disaster-struck unfortunate stumbled out of the tree line, hoping to use the payphone in that parking lot to call for help. Disinterested and having been waiting there too long for too many days, they were not paying a great deal of attention. As the violet shadows lengthened out of the pines across the loose gravel, it became even more difficult to see the stealthy shape that slunk out from beneath the branches.

The figure cut a careful path around the edge of the parking lot, staying shadowed. The pale tubular bulb in the payphone's head shone, a lighthouse in the darkness, its fluorescent white glow glittering on the chrome wheel wells of the huge truck. And then, abruptly, it went out. The women in the truck took notice of this. They exchanged worried glances, and one muttered something into a long range radio. A moment later, the passenger side door of the truck was yanked open, and the radio recorded a brief flurry of violence before the finger holding its button went slack.

A little while later, the two women lay unconscious and bound in the bed of the truck, and there was silence in the darkening parking lot once again. A figure moved from the truck to the now dark but still operational payphone and placed a call.

Back in the forest, Daniel listened to the commotion on the radio and quietly ignored it. This was the last thing he could do for Asher, if the commotion had been him at all, as Daniel suspected. He didn't want to see the man killed, whatever their differences or arguments. He hoped Asher would be able to handle the rest of his escape from here. Daniel had his own path to walk, and it was tied up with Donahue, who he heard returning now, crashing noisily through the brush.

"Alright that's it!" Donahue spat, stomping like an angry toddler, leaves in his hair and brambles caught in his expensive designer hiking gear. This was the third time they'd gone out and come back only for

Daniel to point them in another direction with a hopeless shrug.

"I've had enough!" Donahue was throwing a full blown temper tantrum, throwing his gear on the ground and kicking at bushes. Susan rolled her eyes as, not a hair out of place, she slid liquidly out of the shadows after him.

"Where is he?" Donahue rounded on Daniel, who held up his hands defenselessly. "Where did he go? I don't care if you cannibalized him to survive at this point! Just tell me so we can stop looking!"

"I don't know!" Daniel cowered against his tree helplessly. "We've tried everything I could think of."

"He didn't just disappear." Donahue hissed, "He must have gone somewhere. Try harder!"

Daniel scrunched his nose in thought for a few minutes, then looked up in realization.

"He might have gone back," he suggested, "the way we came. Maybe he regretted the fight, and thought I would too. So he went back somewhere we would both be able to find if we got lost. There was a meadow we camped in just last night. I'm sure he went back there to wait for me to get lost and come back to him."

"Great." Donahue didn't seem any happier, and grabbed Daniel by the arm, yanking him to his feet

"This time you're coming with me. I don't care how long it takes. No mistakes this time."

"Sir, it's getting dark," Susan pointed out. "We should begin heading back. We don't want to become lost ourselves."

"It's not far," Daniel promised, limping ahead. "We hadn't been going more than a couple of hours before we split up. And with both of us injured, we weren't going very fast. We'll find him before full dark. And with your GPS and all your gear, we'll still be able to find our way back out."

"I don't want to be out here another day, Susan." Donahue snarled. "I want this over with tonight!"

"Yes, Mr. Donahue," Susan answered, discontent but with no choice but to comply.

Daniel led them on, heart racing as he realized he might be about to see Asher again. They shouldn't have split up. God, he hoped the other man was alright. He'd been so stupid to argue.

He still had to stop every little while, his ankle sending shooting pains up his leg with every step now. Donahue wouldn't let him rest long, pushing him ahead demandingly, shoving him forward, nearly all pretense of concern gone. Daniel just kept going, heart in his throat, not sure if he hoped Asher wasn't there more than he hoped he was. If he was there, Donahue would try to kill him. But if he wasn't...

192

"Sir," Susan stopped them suddenly, glaring down at her GPS, "we're going in circles."

Donahue turned on Daniel, murder in his eyes. Daniel backed up quickly.

"I'm sorry." he said quickly. "These woods are confusing in the dark!"

"Well you had better get un-confused right now!" Donahue's laugh was anything but cheerful as he took Daniel by the shoulders and shook him, "If I don't see that meathead's corpse in front of me in five minutes—"

"Okay, okay!" Daniel cringed away in fear. "I'm sorry. I've been doing it on purpose. I...I just really don't want to see him again. While we were trying to survive together, we got close. I thought we were, almost... but then as soon as we were about to be rescued he turned into a total asshole again. It was all fake, just to get me to cooperate with him so he could use me to stay alive."

Donahue laughed like a rabid hyena, covering his eyes with his hand.

"Christ, I should have known!" Donahue cackled. "The way he kept flirting with you was so obvious. Well guess what, I don't care if you and your new boyfriend broke up. Just find him. Now!"

Dragging Daniel by his shoulder, Donahue forced the other man forward. Daniel, head low with shame, led Donahue and Susan on towards the meadow, knowing he wouldn't be able to lead them in circles any more now that Susan was watching the GPS like a hawk. It was time for him to face his fears.

"It's just a little further," he promised as they approached the meadow. "It's through this briar."

"Of course it is," Donahue sulked, "Why not walk through a mile of thorns on top of everything else? Why did I ever think this trip was a good idea? Remind me to make the company trip to a sinkhole next time. Much more convenient."

"As long as it isn't anywhere hot, sir," Susan suggested. "You know what the heat does to you."

"Of course, of course," Donahue waved Susan's concern off, trying to yank his pants free of a stubborn thorn. "You'll arrange everything, I'm sure. For the love of shit I will *strangle* whoever came up with thorns!"

"That would be God, sir," Susan said dryly. "According to conventional wisdom anyway."

"Susan! Make a note! I'm going to strangle God."

"Duly noted, sir."

Daniel began to wonder if it was possible to start hallucinating before passing out. He used his stick to flatten another section of bracken and step over it. "Almost there!" he announced excitedly. "I think I can see the clearing!"

He pushed forward eagerly, then froze as he stepped into the small, flower covered circle.

The once vibrant wild flowers had been torn up in violent furrows. Canvas tatters of the sleeping bag were scattered across the grass, waving in the night breeze where they hung from tree branches. The contents of the bag of supplies they'd brought from the cabin were flung wildly in every direction. And at the center of the mess a body was slumped, clothing in ragged tatters, soaked in blood.

Daniel made a strangled, horrified sound and rushed forward as Donahue and Susan climbed through the bramble behind him. He dropped his walking stick and fell to his knees, wordless sounds of distress leaving him as he took Asher's handsome, bloodied face into his hands.

"Looks like a bear attack," Susan murmured, observing the destruction as Daniel, weeping openly, cradled Asher close. "We shouldn't linger here. It will be back."

"Well that's anti-climactic," Donahue sighed as he watched blood seeping into Daniel's clothes from the corpse he held. "We come all this way to kill him and a bear gets to him first? Whatever gets the job done I suppose."

He shrugged and Daniel looked back at him, wide eyed and confused. "Kill him?" Daniel repeated, shaking. "I thought you wanted to save him?"

"God, Carter, for a smart guy, you are unbelievably stupid," Donahue rolled his eyes. "You really thought that guy was a trail guide? Honestly? He's a thug. A hired gun from the mob. He only came out here to hound me about money. And I insisted on this location because of just how many ways something can go wrong and a person can disappear and never be found."

"You were planning to kill him the whole time?" Daniel stared at Donahue, stunned and afraid.

"Of course!" Donahue gave Daniel a look that spelled the word, 'duh!'

"I shouldn't have tried throwing you in the river," he confessed, shrugging. "I didn't anticipate how difficult it would be to find your bodies afterwards. I certainly didn't think you'd *survive*. But it will certainly make covering all of this up easier! You and the meathead will just never be found. The mob will go after him thinking he ran off with the money, and my debts will be erased. A happy ending for everyone."

Daniel clung to Asher's body like he could protect it, horrified. "You're going to kill me too?"

"Carter," Donahue laughed, "why do you think I insisted on you coming on this trip in the first place?

All that digging in financial records you should never have been looking at, whining about attorneys and money disappearing. Did you really not put it together?"

Daniel, stunned, looked down at Asher, shame at his own stupidity seeming to wash over him. "You were embezzling from the company," Daniel concluded. "That's why the finances didn't make sense. Were you just burying the evidence in records?"

"I had someone down there paid to make sure the relevant documents found their way into a furnace," Donahue said, smug, proud of his sloppy work. "I can live as I like on the company funds for now, and if the water ever gets too hot I have millions put away to retire on. If you hadn't been so bone-numbingly stupid, you could have had a cut. But you decided to be a nosy busybody instead. Maybe I'll move Lynda-with-a-y to your desk next. She seems like a lady who can mind her own business."

"Embezzlement, murder, borrowing from the mob..." Daniel, shaking his hanging head in disbelief, sounded awed. "Is there anything else you want to confess before you kill me?"

"Well," Donahue snorted, gesturing Susan forward, "now that you mention it, I also quite enjoy pirating music."

Susan pulled a compact snub nosed pistol as sleek and efficient as she was from underneath her dove gray coat and brought its barrel to bear on Daniel's head with a steady hand.

"Good bye, Mr. Carter," she said in a voice like cold silk.

Daniel looked up at her, a grin and Asher's blood on his face. "Good bye, Susan."

Chapter Twenty

"*Just leave me alone!*"

The cry rang through the forest, startling the birds from their branches. It was still late morning and Daniel, angry tears in his eyes, turned to leave Asher behind.

"Danny, stop!" Asher caught Daniel by the arm and Daniel swung around and punched him, full force, in the nose. Asher stumbled back for a moment, stunned and blinking, his nose pouring blood. Daniel looked as shocked as he was, but then an instant later turned, trying to hurry away. Asher lunged after him and caught him by the arm again.

"Let go!" Daniel demanded as Asher, blood draining down his face, dragged him closer. "Let me go, damn it!"

Asher held him tighter instead, crushing Daniel to his chest until Daniel gave up struggling. Slowly, the fight drained out of him, and Daniel pressed his face to Asher's shoulder as sobs shook him. Slowly, they sank together into the pine needles.

"I want this," Asher said, his voice rough past the blood. "I want to be with you. Yeah you're bitter and weird. But that's part of why I want to be with you. I saw you on that bus alone and I thought you were my type right away. And when we talked and you were so closed off, it was like a game. A challenge I wanted to beat. And then I saw under all that harshness, all your stiff awkward armor, and you were kind, and funny, and one of the bravest men I've ever met. And I thought, I'd better keep this one at arm's length, or I'm going to fall in love."

Daniel tensed in Asher's arms, not daring to look up in case he saw humor in Asher's eyes. If the man wasn't being honest Daniel didn't want to know.

"But I messed up," Asher's voice was soft with tenderness, his lips slick with blood as they pressed against Daniel's forehead. "I couldn't help it. I kept trying to remind myself of what was waiting in the real world. But then you'd smile at me and it would all go away. Please believe me when I say it's not because of you. I don't think I've ever fallen this fast for anyone, extreme situation aside. I just don't want to see you get hurt."

"You don't need to protect me," Daniel's hands tightened in Asher's shirt, fierceness in his voice. "I told you. I'm a man, I can handle it. I don't know what's going to happen or how I'll feel when we get out of here, but I don't want to lose this. I want to try, Asher. I want to at least give it a chance."

Asher squeezed him tighter, clearly tempted. "I can't make any promises," he said, and caught Daniel's chin, tilting his head back to look him in the eye. "I've never had a serious relationship before. I'll probably be awful at it. But you're the first person I've ever even thought about changing things for. And that's got to mean something."

Daniel felt a wild hope rising in his chest, overwhelming and elated. "I'd kiss you," he laughed, "But you're covered in blood."

"Shit," Asher grumbled, scrubbing at his face. "And whose fault is that? I think you broke my nose. Is it straight?"

"Sorry," Daniel grimaced, apologetic, and reached up to pull Asher's nose back into alignment. The other man swore loudly, kicking at the pine needles and squeezing Daniel tightly.

"So what do we do now?" Daniel asked, brow lined with worry as he pulled out a cloth to wipe Asher's face clean. "If we can't run, and we can't go for rescue without Donahue killing you, what do we do?"

Asher frowned in thought, leaning against a tree and holding Daniel against his chest. "I think you were on to something earlier," he said. "About going back to Donahue."

"What?" Daniel sat up, worried. "No, I wouldn't have really done that even when we were arguing. I wouldn't leave you alone out here."

"Glad to hear it," Asher laughed. "Plus, Donahue is totally planning to kill you too. The way he forced you to come on this trip and got you into that boat with me, he definitely has something planned."

"So why do you want me to go back to him?" Daniel asked, confused.

"Because I don't think he'll kill you if he thinks you can lead him to me," Asher stroked his stubble in thought. "Making sure I disappear is definitely his biggest priority. So if you go to him alone, tell him you can lead him to me, you can guide him around in circles for hours."

"While you get to the trail head and the phones?" Daniel guessed.

"Exactly," Asher nodded, "I'll call in some back up while you keep Donahue preoccupied. And keep an eye on his radio in case I get spotted. I know he'll have someone watching the trail head that I'll need to get around."

"I'm pretty sure I can keep him going in circles till sundown," Daniel agreed, frowning. "He's not the brightest. Susan might be a problem though."

"Sundown should be long enough," Asher was frowning in thought. "When you can't delay him anymore, bring him to the meadow we camped in this morning. I'll figure something out and be there for you."

"And you're sure splitting up is a good idea?" Daniel asked. "We can't just run away together?"

"Even if we could, would you really be okay with letting him go after what he's done?" Asher asked. "I don't know about you, but I want to see him dealt with."

Daniel nodded, still worried, but accepting that this was the best plan. "Alright," he said, taking a deep breath. "Go over the details with me one more time."

Instead, Asher kissed Daniel warmly. Daniel was surprised, but not the least bit displeased, returning the kiss fondly.

"What was that for?" he asked when Asher pulled away.

"I'm just really glad that, if I had to get lost in the woods with someone, it was with you," Asher smiled and brushed Daniel's hair back from his cheek, "I don't think I could have made it with anyone else."

Daniel blushed and looked away, embarrassed by Asher's frank confession and too shy still to state his own feelings out loud. "Right," he mumbled, red faced, "Let's go over the plan again..."

"Goodbye, Susan."

Susan stared down at Daniel, wrinkling her nose in confusion, only to jerk her weapon up as lights flared on in the dense thicket surrounding them. An armed police officer in a vest stepped forward, his gun trained on Susan.

"Drop your weapon and step back."

Around them, more officers were coming out of the trees, surrounding the clearing, their weapons trained on Susan and Donahue. Susan narrowed her calculating gaze down the sight of her little pistol at the nearest officer.

"Susan," Donahue's voice was sharp, then more casual, laughing, "do as the officer says. There's no reason to get defensive. We haven't done anything wrong. This is all just a misunderstanding."

"I've got a verbal confession here that says you did a lot of wrong, Donahue."

Asher sat up in Daniel's arms, holding up the police issue body camera he'd had trained on them during the entirety of Donahue's little speech.

To Donahue's credit, he only looked shocked for a moment to see that Asher was still alive. Then he merely looked disgusted.

"I should have guessed you were faking. That seems to be most of your personality."

"I'm a complicated guy," Asher said with a roguish grin. "You figured it out pretty fast, Daniel. What gave me away?"

"I've been eating those MREs for days," Daniel laughed. "I'd recognize the smell of that spaghetti anywhere."

Asher shrugged and wiped a gob of sauce off of his shirt.

"We were working under a bit of a time crunch. Luckily it's pretty hard to tell spaghetti sauce from blood in the dark like this."

"Hey! Stop!"

Asher's head whipped around as one of the officers shouted. Susan darted for an opening in the men surrounding them and, reluctant to fire on her, she vanished past them into the tree line. There was a quick exchange of orders and several men went after her, the rest remaining behind to put cuffs on Donahue. Daniel watched her go, worried, but Asher just shook his head. Susan was only a hired gun. With Donahue out of the picture, she was harmless.

"That will never hold up in court," Donahue was cool as a cucumber, calmly allowing himself to be arrested. "My lawyers will tear you apart."

"I think it'll be enough," Asher replied, standing up and helping Daniel to his feet. "Especially once we add the proof of embezzlement Daniel found. Not to mention all the evidence I collected on your work with the mob."

Donahue began to look nauseous. He eyed the way Susan had run off, considering, but the police only tightened their grip on him and began to pull him away.

"Uh, speaking of that," Daniel cut in, looking at the police around them, "when you said backup, I wasn't really expecting the police."

"Yeah," Asher looked away guiltily, "I may have been stretching the truth a little when I said I was just a thug. I am. Because I was placed there undercover by the organized crime unit. I really wasn't kidding when I said my life was dangerous..."

Daniel laughed, a weird kind of relief rushing through him.

"Thank God," he sighed, leaning against Asher's side. "Don't get me wrong. I was willing to try this thinking you were a criminal. But I'm very glad you aren't."

Asher smiled, and Daniel wished he could kiss the other man. Neither dared while there were so many people watching. But Daniel's heart sped up at that smile, knowing as soon as they could be alone he would have all he wanted. He'd been genuinely terrified for a minute there, seeing Asher on the ground like that. Once he'd figured out what was going on, he'd done his best to get Donahue to confess to as much as possible. It wasn't difficult to get someone as self-absorbed as Donahue monologuing. But seeing Asher that way, even for a second, had made him all the more certain he didn't want to be without the other man, ever again.

Chapter Twenty-One

A police ATV carried Asher and Daniel out of the forest and back to the Cow Creek Trailhead. They sat in the parking lot under the bright light of police flood lamps, wearing stress blankets and waiting for an ambulance to arrive. They both gave statements, and Daniel was as honest as possible while glossing over his relationship with Asher. He still wasn't sure he'd completely come to terms with being gay himself. He certainly wasn't ready to start announcing it to the public and Asher's coworkers. Some of them, he felt, guessed. Or maybe he was just being paranoid.

They stayed close to each other throughout everything, each reluctant to let the other leave his sight. Now that it was all over, Daniel felt the beginnings of a kind of numbness creeping over him. Shock or something, probably. The worry of how he would survive was easing away, and soon the worry of how he would live would take its place, and between them a dull void where he simply existed and was glad. In celebration of the achievement of surviving, he allowed himself the risk of leaning against Asher's side, resting his head on the other man's shoulder. Asher smiled down at him, checked to make sure no one was looking, then pressed a kiss to the top of his head. Daniel wanted this to last forever.

It was taking awhile for the ambulance to arrive, presumably due to the remoteness and the fact that neither man was in critical condition. The squad car carrying Donahue to his justice had long since left and things had quieted down. Only a small escort remained, keeping an eye on the two injured men and cleaning up a last few details of the scene.

"Investigating this is going to be a bitch," Asher confided. I do not envy the guy who gets stuck with that job."

Daniel nodded, eyes half closed. He was really looking forward to the 'sleep for a week' portion of the plan. Asher shifted and Daniel sat up, blinking the sleep from his eyes.

"Want to, uh, go look for the bathrooms with me?" Asher suggested, waggling his eyebrows in a salacious fashion.

Daniel snorted. "Shouldn't we stay put?" he asked. "The ambulance."

"Just for a minute," Asher insisted. "They won't even notice we're gone."

Daniel grinned, unable to resist, and the two men slid off the hood of the cop car they'd been sitting on and slunk together towards the shadow of a ranch house.

The building was unlocked, the police having used it to plan their rescue, but the interior was dusty and eerie with a sense of abandonment. The house dated back to the 1800's, but even in the busier season its little museum was not a huge draw. Its rooms were cast in deep, sepia shadow, timeless shelter of secret romances. The two men did not go far in before Asher pinned Daniel to a wall and kissed him hard, as though they'd been separated a week rather than a few hours.

"You still smell like tomato sauce," Daniel laughed when Asher broke the kiss. "I think you're going to need a shower before I can go much further with you."

"I think I can change your mind," Asher teased, dropping kisses down Daniel's throat, knowing how that ruined Daniel's willpower. "Who knows? It might be so amazing you can't eat spaghetti without thinking of me ever again."

Daniel laughed, breathless and hushed, afraid to be overheard and caught. His laughter became a moan as Asher's teeth grazed the sweet spot where his throat met his shoulder. The other man's hands ran down to catch Daniel by his thighs and lift him, pressing him against the wall. Daniel hooked a leg around Asher's hip, eager for the friction it brought, while his hands clawed at Asher's shirt, pulling it up to run his palms over the powerful muscles of Asher's back.

Asher squeezed at Daniel's ass, pulling the smaller man's hips against his. They rutted against each other in their rush to be as close as possible, to touch each other as much as they could. As Asher kissed him again, Daniel began to really hope for the first time that this might really work. Before, the hope had been so wild and distant, he might as well have been hoping for his fairy godmother to appear and make his dreams come true. Now it seemed actually possible. Not just a beautiful dream, but a reality he could actually see taking shape as his lips moved against Asher's. They could really be together. The thought made him so happy he thought his heart would leap right out of his chest. He wondered if this was what love felt like.

He heard a creak behind Asher and froze. Before he could react any further than that, an awful crack resounded through the old house. Asher's eyes widened in front of Daniel, then rolled back in his head. He slumped, revealing Susan standing behind him with a pistol and a police baton. Daniel caught the other man, staring at Susan in wide eyed shock.

"Grab him." Susan ordered, her pistol pointed at Daniel. "And follow me. Move!"

She didn't look the least bit flustered by her flight from the police, still as sleek and dangerous as ever. Daniel, terrified, obeyed, wrapping his arms around the unconscious Asher and pulling him along as Susan led them deeper into the house.

"The police are right outside," Daniel reminded her. "You should be focusing on getting away. Just let us go and run for it while you have the chance."

"They aren't even looking for you yet," Susan said with utter, unflappable confidence. "I have plenty of time."

She led them back through the house to a set of stairs, descending down beneath the house. She removed a chain and sign warning visitors to stay out. She gestured with the gun for him to go down. Daniel felt an anxious pit growing in his stomach, opening up like a sink hole.

"Why are you even doing this?" Daniel asked as he pulled Asher down the stairs. "Why bother?"

"Revenge, mostly." Susan replied, calm and almost disinterested as she followed them down into the basement, flipping a switch that illuminated a bare single bulb down below. Its faded orange light was not comforting. "I really liked that job. Donahue was a greedy idiot, but he was a useful greedy idiot. I was taking millions out from under him while he took all the risk. It was a fantastic set up and you ruined it. On top of that, those records you found could reveal my accounts as well. If you're dead, it will take the police longer to find them. I'll have time to clear out my accounts and set myself up somewhere new, with another greedy idiot to use."

The basement was mostly empty concrete and a set of washing machines. Just a storage area for the maintenance people. There was no way out through here.

"I told Donahue not to borrow from the mob," Susan sighed in frustration. "I told him this killing you in the mountains thing was stupid too. He should have just let me handle it. You would have quietly committed suicide in your apartment and Price would have disappeared for a while, then turned up dead under an overpass with a needle in his arm. Much more efficient. Next time, I'll get a more easily manipulated idiot."

Daniel pulled Asher into the center of the dimly lit room, beneath the bare orange bulb with its baleful red glow. He stared up at Susan and her gun, searching for a way, any way, out of this.

"Don't you think killing a cop will just make things more difficult for you?" he tried. "They'll come after you with everything. You could still just leave now and get away."

"Don't be ridiculous," Susan scoffed, checking her pistol for how many rounds she had left. "I'm going to make it look like you did it, of course."

Daniel's blood felt like ice water in his veins. "I'm the only one you need to kill, right?" he said, voice shaking as he stood over the unconscious man. "In order to get away like you want to? So just leave Asher. You don't need the extra heat. Just kill me and leave."

Susan rolled her eyes.

"Very brave," she commended, checking her watch, "But in case you forgot, I'm also looking for revenge. Now go and stand by the stairs. I want to make it look like you lured him down here and shot him in the back."

Daniel did as he was told, stomach turning with panic. He had to find some way out of this. He stood in front of the stairs as Susan calculated the angle she needed to shoot Asher at.

"Just relax," she said, adjusting his position. "It'll all be over soon."

Daniel turned suddenly, tilting his head towards the stairs. "Did you hear that?" he asked.

Susan clicked her tongue impatiently. "As though I'd fall for—"

"Price? Carter? You two in here?" a loud voice called from the other end of the house, near the front doors.

"Help!" Daniel shouted at once. "Down here!"

"Shit." Susan muttered and raised her gun on Daniel, finger closing on the trigger, ready to end this quickly now that she was out of time.

Asher collided with her an instant later and Daniel felt the wind of her bullet past his ear as she fired. The noise was deafening in the concrete basement, leaving Daniel stunned, watching Asher pin the ferocious woman to the stairs, grappling to try and get the gun away from her. Daniel saw another officer at the top of the stairs, frozen, unable to fire without risking hitting Asher.

Asher got a lucky blow in and the gun skittered away across the basement floor as the two rolled over, striking at each other with wild, furious blows. Susan's hand was around Asher's neck, white knuckled as she dug her fingers into his carotid artery. Asher was losing strength, struggling to stay conscious between her grip and the earlier blow to his head. He held out, fighting valiantly.

For the first time, as Asher swung at her, Daniel saw Susan looking less than perfectly composed, her hair torn loose from its efficient bun by his fingers, her teeth clenched in animal rage, her glasses askew. How outraged she would have been to know it was the last expression she'd wear.

"Now!" Daniel shouted, and Asher shoved Susan away as hard as he could. Daniel, holding her dropped pistol, pointed it at her and squeezed the trigger until the thunder stopped ringing in his ears and, through the roaring tinnitus, an empty clicking was all he heard. Susan lay against the far basement wall, dead or close enough that it hardly mattered. Daniel threw the pistol away quickly, disgusted, and hurried to Asher's side. The other police officers were crowding the stairs as Daniel pulled the blond man to his feet, helping him stay upright as he wobbled. They clung to each other unself-consciously as they answered the other officer's questions. Things were about to get very busy again. Daniel didn't care. They were alive. They were together. The rest of the world could go hang.

Chapter Twenty-Two

They were airlifted out by police helicopter and taken to the nearest hospital, their injuries finally properly treated. Daniel was thoroughly scolded for making his ankle worse by walking on it so long, and apparently the fact that he'd managed to keep going with so many hairline fractures ("Just everywhere, really," according to an x-ray technician) was pretty impressive. Asher joked that Daniel should join the force, but Daniel was genuinely looking forward to going back to a desk job. They shared a hospital room, on their insistence, as they both recuperated, but after a few days they were both well enough to finish healing at home. There was an awkward moment as they stood in the hospital waiting room, trying to figure out where they would go, and if they would go there together.

"Do you live in Colorado?" Asher asked. "I don't even know where you come from."

"I'm from out of state," Daniel confirmed, suddenly worried this might be the end, after all they'd been through. "What about you?"

"Originally from Florida," he admitted. "I have a place here in Colorado, but I can't go back there now that my cover is blown. The department will probably relocate me."

"If you need a place to stay," Daniel offered, suddenly hopeful. "I've got the space."

Asher's eyes brightened and for a moment Daniel thought he would accept. But then he seemed to remember himself. He looked away, shaking his head. "Thanks," he said, "but the department wants me to stay close till this whole mess is sorted out."

"Oh." Daniel's shoulders sank, and he looked down at the scuffed tile floor, watching his hopes slowly wilt. He had known this would happen, but he still hadn't been ready for it.

"Yeah." Asher looked at least as miserable as Daniel felt, staring away down the hall like it held the answers that would keep them together. The truth was that they knew practically nothing about each other. Nothing practical anyway. Addresses, birthdays, family, favorite foods, taste in movies, all the little parts and pieces that made up a real relationship. Daniel knew how strong Asher was. How kind he could be, even when in pain and under terrible stress. The way he joked to hide how he was feeling. The way he played with his hair when he was lying. The piercing intensity of his eyes when he was being sincere. Daniel knew all these details. But he'd only just learned the man was born in Florida. And maybe that just wasn't enough to make a relationship on.

"Did you get your cell phone back?"

Daniel looked up as Asher spoke and nodded in confirmation, pulling the device out of his bag.

"Can I have your number?" Asher asked, pulling out his phone as well. "So that we can—you know. Once everything is settled."

"Of course," Daniel agreed at once, and they exchanged numbers quickly. It gave Daniel a little hope, this concrete thread of Asher's presence in his life that he could hold on to.

A taxi pulled up in front of the hospital, waiting to take Daniel to the airport.

"I'll call you soon," Asher promised, "So wait for me, okay? Don't go running off with any handsome cab drivers or anything."

Daniel laughed a little, shook his head and, without even checking to see if they were alone, leaned up to kiss Asher on the cheek. "Thank you," he said, in case he never got another chance, "for everything."

"I should be thanking you," Asher murmured, his eyes full of longing. "You saved me out there. In more ways than I can name."

The taxi honked outside and Daniel pulled away reluctantly. "I had better go," he said. "Don't get killed by the mob while I'm not around to save you."

"No promises," Asher laughed as Daniel headed for the door, glancing back often. "I'll see you soon. Don't get eaten by any bears!"

"No promises!" Daniel called back, smiling bittersweet as the hospital doors closed between them. The words 'I love you' sat unsaid like a cold lump in his throat. He climbed into the cab and wondered if that was the last thing he would ever say to Asher.

His phone rang and Daniel fumbled to answer it, confused. "Hello?" he asked, not checking to see who it was.

"Told you I'd call soon!" Asher said on the other end. Daniel looked up to see him waving through the glass doors of the hospital. "You're not gonna be busy for a few hours while you wait for your flight, right? How about I keep you company?"

Daniel smiled, watching Asher as the cab pulled away until he couldn't see the other man's face any more, then he leaned his head back against the seat and closed his eyes, overwhelmed with happiness.

"That sounds great," he answered, voice a little rough with emotion. "So. Uh, tell me about where you grew up?"

A few months later, Daniel was back in his quiet apartment. It didn't feel so empty anymore. Daniel had bought that fish. It was only a betta for now, bright scarlet with streaming fins. He figured he'd work his way up to something bigger. A potted cactus sat beside the fish tank, a welcome home gift from

Lynda and everyone at the office. He was trying to be less closed off, and his coworkers had responded to the new him with open arms. He was going bowling with a couple of them this weekend.

The office itself had passed into the hands of one of Donahue's relatives, a sober and far more reliable man, who'd vowed to make sure no one lost their jobs while the company was under investigation for Donahue's crimes. Daniel had even been given a small raise for spotting Donahue's financial chicanery early. It wasn't much, but it was all Daniel needed. He was, for the most part, content.

He talked to Asher nearly every day. Asher joked that he had nothing better to do since the department had him sitting on his hands until the case was wrapped up. They talked about Asher's family and Daniel's childhood and what schools they had gone to and what movies they loved and what food they hated and, with rare exception, found they complemented each other well. All the little details of their lives had begun to fill in for each other. Now Daniel knew he got that habit of playing with his hair when he lied from his mother, and that when he was a kid he'd wanted to be a comedian, and had practiced jokes with his brothers. The knowledge had illuminated and embellished on what he already knew, painting a richer picture. If possible, Daniel thought he liked Asher even more. He could only hope the other man felt the same upon learning more about him.

Daniel fed his fish, which he'd named Charlemagne, while a cooking show chattered blithely in the background of a peaceful, empty afternoon. For once Daniel didn't feel antsy or eager to leave the still apartment. It was about the time of day when Asher usually called him, and looking forward to it made the apartment feel not empty, but full of potential.

Just as he was putting down the fish food his phone rang, and he rushed to answer it. "Asher!" he said, smile audible as he picked up his phone. "I was hoping you would call soon. How was—"

He was interrupted by the sound of his apartment doorbell ringing. He frowned, wondering who would be visiting right now. "Sorry, one second," he said. "There's someone at the door."

Still holding the phone to his ear he hurried across the living room to open the front door.

Asher stood on the other side, holding his phone. He smiled. "Hey Danny."

Daniel threw himself forward before he knew what he was doing, hugging Asher tightly and pulling the other man into the apartment.

"What are you doing here?" he asked, elated. "Did the department finally let you go?"

"One better than that," Asher replied. "They approved my relocation. I'm moving here."

Daniel just stared at him, stunned, for a moment. "Are you... are you moving in here?" he asked, a little thrown.

Asher laughed. "No, no, I've got my own place," he said. "It seemed a little early in the relationship to be moving in together."

"Yeah, I guess so," Daniel laughed. "I just can't believe you're finally here."

"I couldn't wait to see you," Asher reached out to touch Daniel's hair, combing it back behind his ear. "I've missed you... And I wanted to ask you something."

"Anything," Daniel said at once. "How can I help?"

Asher laughed, shaking his head. "I wanted to ask you," he said, slow and a little nervous. "If you would like to go on a date with me? I figured, since we had never really been on one, it might be a good place to start. We could see a movie, get dinner." He looked at Daniel with big, hopeful eyes, as though there were any chance Daniel would turn him down.

"I'd love that," Daniel replied, grinning from ear to ear. "I would really, really love that."

He pulled Asher down and kissed him, all the affection he'd been holding back bubbling over all at once. Asher didn't resist, pulling Daniel close and returning the kiss with a passion that said he'd been holding back for a long time too. Daniel stepped backwards and his knees hit the back the couch. He stumbled, falling backwards, but Asher caught him, turning it into a controlled descent. He knelt over Daniel, fingers sliding under the smaller man's shirt as his kisses drifted down to Daniel's throat.

"We'll miss the movie," Daniel teased as Asher pushed up his shirt to kiss his way down Daniel's chest.

"There's a later showing," Asher said quickly, tossing Daniel's shirt away and pulling at his own pants.

"What about dinner?" Daniel giggled, unbuckling Asher's belt with deft fingers.

"I think I'd rather have dessert first." Asher replied, leaning back on his knees as Daniel worked his pants open.

Daniel licked his lips, looking up at Asher with mischievous eyes. "Me too."

Asher was already half hard and Daniel swallowed the other man with vigor and an eye towards showing him exactly how much he'd been missed. He knew he should take things slow and build Asher up first, but he was too excited by the man's very presence. He wanted to do everything all at once.

Asher bent forward with a stammering groan as Daniel engulfed him, mouth hot and eager, moving at a pace that had Asher cursing and grabbing for Daniel's head to slow him down, lest this end far too fast. He planted a hand on the arm rest behind Daniel, bending over him, shifting forward to straddle him better. Daniel held still despite his impatience, obeying the hand in his hair that was holding him in place. He expected Asher to let go and allow Daniel to resume in a moment, once he had his control back. Instead, Asher kept his hold on Daniel's head and began to slowly move his hips, rocking into Daniel's mouth. Daniel was surprised but not unreceptive, relaxing and allowing Asher to fuck his mouth at his own speed.

Asher went at a slow, deliberate pace, cradling Daniel's head and taking great care not to hurt the other man even as he used him. Daniel closed his eyes and focused on keeping his jaw and throat relaxed, making it easy for Asher to slide deeper. Asher gave a wordless moan of approval, stroking Daniel's hair.

"That's it," he murmured. "Just like that. Tilt your head back a little further. You're so good at this, Danny."

The praise sent a thrill through Daniel almost as pleasant as the guilty delight of being used this way. He slid a hand down underneath Asher to stroke himself through his pants, too hard just from this situation to go on ignoring himself.

"Just a little more," Asher was breathless, grinding deeper into Daniel's throat. "God, your mouth feels so good."

Daniel moaned around Asher's cock as the other man sank deeper into his throat, holding his breath until his vision began to darken at the edges and his thoughts began to float and disconnect, his body tingling. Still Asher rocked into him, and then suddenly stopped, babbling Daniel's name amid curses, and Daniel felt the hot rush of cum in his throat. He was still rubbing himself frantically through his pants, and as Asher pulled out and air flooded back into Daniel's lungs like fire, lighting him up, his hips jerked upwards and he felt himself tumbling over the edge of orgasm all at once.

He was left stunned, lying against the couch in surprise mingled with embarrassment at how strongly he'd reacted to that, while Asher fell back against the opposite side of the couch to catch his breath.

"Fuck," Daniel said after a long moment, his voice rough. "I'm going to have to change my pants."

"Sorry," Asher was still coming down, his words breathy and euphoric. "I got carried away there."

"No apology necessary," Daniel laughed though his throat hurt. His entire body was still prickling with excitement. He looked up to catch Asher's eye across the couch and spread his legs, revealing the wet spot where his cum was soaking through, "Want to make the movie a very late showing?"

"Absolutely."

Chapter Twenty-Three

They never did make the movie. Once Daniel gave in to Asher's request to 'try something,' there was no chance they'd leave the apartment that night. He bound and blindfolded Daniel in his own silk work ties and spent hours working him up with soft sensory teasing before taking him. And then again in the shower, and then again in the kitchen, making up for all the months apart. They slowed down in the weeks and months that followed, if only because if they'd continued at that pace, neither of them would ever have slept nor eaten.

Great as the sex was, Daniel liked the quiet moments more. The early mornings after nights when Asher slept over, when he'd make coffee and they'd talk idly over breakfast. Or late at night, when he woke and found the other man beside him. All his feelings of loneliness had disappeared.

It was just such a quiet moment now, the sun just risen, the morning soft and silver with the early light. Mist moved through the trees, the tops of their highest boughs just barely touched with gold. Steam curled up from Daniel's coffee cup as he leaned back on the porch swing, watching the slide of bright colors over the sides of the blue shaded mountains in the distance. The dawn chorus of spring song birds was rising musically all around the isolated cabin. Daniel sighed in peaceful contentment.

Though their relationship had started in an unusual way, they'd been dating properly for almost a year when they took their first vacation together. Asher had suggested going back to the Rockies as a joke at first, but Daniel had found the idea stuck with him. Eventually they'd agreed it was only right to revisit the place that had brought them together. Though this cabin was significantly nicer than the abandoned ranger station, with electricity and air conditioning and a store just a short drive away in Asher's truck.

Looking out from its little patio, however, Daniel could see Mummy Mountain, where the cabin they'd sheltered in must still be, closed up again now, filling with dust, waiting for another stranded hiker to rescue. Daniel wished they had left something there. Some way to mark what the place had done for them. But at the same time, that wasn't a hike he felt like making again.

He heard the door open behind him as Asher stepped outside, yawning and holding his own coffee, looking sleep mussed and perfect in a loose t-shirt and sweatpants. He sank onto the bench next to Daniel, and Daniel didn't hesitate to curl up against him, happy to share this morning with him. A little while after he'd started dating Daniel seriously, Asher had stopped accepting undercover assignments, alleviating Daniel's worries about his safety and allowing him to be around for the other man more regularly. He'd been doing well in spite of this and was close to making detective.

"You looked so solemn out here by yourself," Asher said, kissing the top of Daniel's head. "It reminded me of the first time I saw you. What were you thinking about?"

"Just remembering that cabin," Daniel explained, smiling. "I was so scared back then. I still don't know if I was more scared of it being real or just a result of the situation we were in. No, I think that's wrong. I was scared as hell of it being real and having to change my life. But I was more scared of going back to being alone."

"Any regrets?" Asher asked. "An anniversary like this is a good time to review."

Daniel thought about it seriously for a moment, then shook his head. "Not really," he said. "Well, maybe that one thing with your parents."

Asher laughed, squeezing him closer.

"What about you?" Daniel's heart sped up, still a little insecure after all this time, unable to believe someone like Asher could really want to be with someone like him. "Any regrets?"

"Not a one," Asher said without hesitation, smiling down at Daniel in undisguised adoration. "I want to be with you for the rest of my life, Danny."

Daniel blushed and hid his face in Asher's arm, still not used to how easily the other man could say such embarrassing things.

"I love you Asher," he said, though he couldn't meet Asher's eye as he said it. He'd only found the courage to start saying it at all recently.

"I love you too, Daniel," Asher replied, soft and sincere, and pulled him into a kiss just as the sun broke over the horizon and spilled golden light over the cabin, the patio, and the two lovers curled up together, alone among nature, needing nothing but each other.

Made in the USA
Middletown, DE
04 September 2016